GHOST IN THE SPELL

Grimoires of a Middle-aged Witch Book 5

RENEE GEORGE

Barkside of the Moon Press

Ghost in the Spell

Grimoires of a Middle-aged Witch Book 5

Publisher: Barkside of the Moon Press

Print ISBN: 978-1-947177-47-5

For Robbin & Robyn

ACKNOWLEDGMENTS

I have to thank the usual people for helping me get to the end of this book.

First, Robbin Clubb and Robyn Peterman, my critique partners, know just when to kick my ass when I need it! Thank you, Lindas!

Second, to the readers and my Rebels, without you all, what would be the point? I am so happy and blessed to have you guys in my corner!

Third, thank you, Mitra! You know why.

Forth but not least, coffee. Thank you, strong black coffee, for giving me the energy to bring this baby home. You are the miracle in my life.

Fifth, my newly discovered muse-kickstarter, Beethoven! I wore my headphones non-stop, and I wouldn't have been able to focus without you, maestro!

Being a forty-something divorcee with a college-bound teenage son is a freaking cakewalk compared to wielding my unruly magic.

Did I mention that my newly discovered sister wants to kill me?

After a hellish week spent with older-than-dirt arch-druids and a few new enemies, I'm ready to get home so I can hug my kid and sleep in my own bed. But nope, that's not how my crazy magical mid-life works. My spirit magic has been triggered, and a ghost's cryptic message gives me more bad news. Something worse than my psycho sister might be after me. Awesome.

It's Battle Royale time. I'm so over selfish magical creatures trying to steal my powers and my life. I'll need the help of all my tru-craft guardians if I stand a chance against my supernatural foes. But first, I'll have to get into the spirit of my new element before the spirit gets into me.

Literally.

CHAPTER 1

BEWARE THE FATHER.

The ominous warning haunted me. What had the bronze lady meant?

Whatever it had been, I couldn't get those three words out of my head.

They ranked right up there with three other terrible words, *Well-played, sister.*

When Bogmall had whispered that sentence in my head, I'd nearly crapped myself. It couldn't be true, could it? Could the blonde hexen-bitch really be my sister? I didn't want to believe it, but something inside me knew it wasn't a lie. Bogmall and I were tied to each other, and not just in the mortal enemy kind of way.

She had connected telepathically with me during the nero-craft test at Iron Grove. The test that should've killed me.

Poor, poor, Iris. Always one step behind me, she'd cooed. *Just like the day we were born.*

We were born. Could she really be my sister? My twin?

Had our mother given her up for adoption as well? It seemed too awful to consider. And while her revelatory words had thrown me for a loop, she hadn't stopped there.

Always the favorite, she'd added. *Always the one that had to be saved no matter the cost. But not anymore. I have my own magic now, and I will have what rightfully should've been mine in the first place. And the minute you take your last breath, that's when I will take you, and I will rot your relationships with everyone and everything that you love.*

The way she'd looked at Keir had made my stomach turn. She had been coming for me with an obsessive fervor for months, and she wasn't done with me yet. Not by a long shot. I'd been on the defense when it came to the hexen-bitch, spending all my time countering her moves, but not anymore. It was time to go on the offense. I would track her down to the ends of the earth and destroy her with my bare hands if it meant keeping my friends and family safe from harm.

Keir planned to research the crap out of Bogmall's history when we got home. If anyone could find out her origin story, it was my bookworm boyfriend. For now, getting back to Southill Village, to my house, to my kid, and to my own bed was priority number one. After the grueling elemental tests, my body hurt as much as my brain, and I needed a couple of days to recover before I went to war.

The car ride home from Iron Grove had been somber. I'd nestled Goldie, the poor goldfish from my ignis-craft test, in the backseat between our bags. Bob, my big cuddly, chonky-chonky, sat in my lap the entire time instead of disappearing like he usually did. Since he didn't talk, I wasn't sure where he went when he wasn't with me, but I was ever so grateful that he managed to show up whenever I needed him the most.

Keir and Linda, my violent gnome whom I adored, had both told me Bob was an imp, a witch's familiar, and more to the point, my familiar. However, it turned out that not every tru-craft witch had one. It was something I'd meant to talk to Thomas about, but from the moment I'd met the man in person at Iron Grove, chaos had reigned. Not his fault, mind you, but circumstances hadn't allowed us much room for shop talk.

Bob appeared in the guise of a giant orange and white cat with a bobbed tail. He weighed at least thirty pounds, but it was thirty pounds of pure love. Since a circle, the symbol for spirit element, appeared on the cover of my Grimoire, Bob had not left my side. Which meant my cortisol levels had to be through the roof. Bob only showed up when I was stressed out or in danger.

I guess finding out I had a psychopathic sister, a new element, and a puzzling warning from a ghost lady was enough to keep Bob nearby. On top of that, and maybe the most distressing, Linda was still missing. I was pretty freaked out that she hadn't returned to me since the fight with the snotgurgle, a monster as gross as its name.

After Keir and I had freed Linda from the troll, the last thing I'd said to her was *run*. The fact that she hadn't run back to the Iron Grove compound concerned me. She'd had several chunks of her body missing when she'd burrowed into the ground and made her escape. Zev had used his djinn powers to scan the area where she'd disappeared and found nothing.

I prayed that she'd made it back to Southill Village and that she'd be home by the time I arrived.

Instead, I was greeted by Evan Callahan, my ex-husband. Not the person I wanted to see.

"What are you doing here?" I held Goldie's fishbowl in my arms.

Evan's face registered surprise. His curly blond hair and dimples gave his face a boyish charm. "Is that a goldfish?" His voice was incredulous.

"Winner winner, chicken dinner." I brushed past him into the living room but left the door open for Keir. He was getting our bags out of the back of the car. I narrowed my gaze at my former husband. "You still haven't answered my question."

The couch had a pillow and a rumpled quilt on the cushions. Good. Evan hadn't been sleeping in my bed. I had been half-afraid I'd have to de-ex-ify my awesomely comfy mattress with the rest of my white sage stash.

My ex-husband looks chagrined. "I don't know, Iris. I just thought it'd be nice to spend a couple of days with my son."

I looked around the living room. "I don't see Michael anywhere, so...?" I let the question hang.

"It's Friday. A school day, Iris." Evan shrugged. "I made him breakfast and sent him on his way."

"That still doesn't answer the mystery of why you're still here,"

"Someone should be here."

I swear I nearly gave myself whiplash the way I spun

around at him. "Are you sure that's the road you want to travel?"

His eyes widened, and his hands went up. "Absolutely not."

Keir came in with my luggage. "I'll take this back to your room," he said as he passed between Evan and me.

Evan arched a brow at Keir as he walked down the hall. "I guess it's getting serious, huh?"

I sighed. "It's serious."

"Like marriage serious?"

"Evan." I shook my head. "My personal life is none of your business."

"We share a son."

"Who's practically an adult." I set Goldie on the coffee table and threw my purse onto the couch. "Besides, Michael likes Keir."

Evan shrugged. "So he says."

"See." I rolled my hand at him. "All is well. Go back to St. Louis."

"I can't."

I will not set my ex-husband on fire became my new mantra. "I thought Adam asked you to marry him. Did you blow it already?"

"No." He sucked his teeth. "I didn't blow it. We're still engaged."

"Congrats." I sat down next to my purse. "I'm happy for you." I couldn't muster the feeling behind the words, but the fact that I had said them had to count for something.

"Thank you." Evan ran his hand over his soft curls and shook his head. "I'm sorry. I'm not trying to start a fight."

"Could've fooled me," I muttered as I tapped Goldie's bowl. The little goldfish swished its tail at me. I was going to have to get a real fish tank and food for her. Or was it him? Later, I would Google how to sex a goldfish.

Evan pretended he didn't hear me. "I only stayed because I'm worried about Michael."

I pivoted my gaze from the fish to my ex. "Why?"

"He has been acting...strange." He shook his head. "Distant. Like he's keeping secrets. Secrets that are eating away at him."

"You mean, like catching his father cheating on his mom?"

"Low blow, Iris."

"Hah. You're not the injured party, Evan." I waved a hand at him dismissively. "So don't play the victim."

It was his turn to sigh. "Can we agree to talk about Michael without getting personal?"

I was through caring about what had or hadn't happened to end our marriage. Besides, if Evan hadn't fallen in love with someone else, my life with Keir would be very different. At the heart of the matter, I was happier now with Keir than I'd ever been with Evan. Still, I was too exhausted for this conversation, and I fantasized about the floor opening and swallowing Evan whole.

"What are your concerns?"

"He's been...distant. Secretive. And, well, two nights ago, he was shouting for someone to stop and to not hurt her, whoever *her* is. When I checked on him, he was thrashing around in his sleep. And when I woke him up, he was shaking." Evan peered at me. "Shaking. I think something happened to him, but he won't talk to me."

My heart squeezed. Michael had witnessed a wraith trying to kill me more than once. Had that been the catalyst for his nightmare?

I rubbed my temples. "I'll talk to him."

"We," Evan gestured between us, "should talk to him together."

Keir came out of the bedroom. "Everything okay?"

Hardly, I thought. Aloud, I said, "Yes, fine." I gestured to my ex. "He's worried about Michael."

Keir's brow furrowed. "Anything I can help with?"

"No." I shook my head. "We're good." I was eager to find out if Linda had returned, so I gave him another way he could help me. "Can you check on the garden?"

"I'll do it now," Keir replied.

I couldn't tell Evan about my tru-craft powers. I might have trusted him once, but those days were long gone. Still, as Michael's father, he deserved some kind of explanation. I gave him half a truth. "Maybe it has something to do with his girlfriend."

Evan's eyes widened. "He has a girlfriend?"

Keir arched his brow at me on his way out but didn't get involved.

"He did," I said. "Sort of. A cheerleader. He saw her for a little while. Then her mother abruptly moved the two of them out of town. I think he's heartbroken." It wasn't a complete lie. Michael really liked Maddie. And her mother, once I'd exercised a diabolical spirit out of her, had packed up her daughter and left town.

"I suppose that could be it." He looked relieved, and it dawned on me that this wasn't a typical Evan move. He really had been worried about Michael.

Until he'd been caught in his web of lies and deceit, he'd been a good dad and, for all appearances, a good husband. I sometimes forgot that. On top of that, he'd been making a real effort to mend his and Michael's relationship, and I didn't want to hinder their progress. I might want Evan out of my life, but I didn't want him out of our son's.

"I'll talk to him." I gave him a sympathetic look. "I promise I'll keep you up to date, and if he's having a really rough time, I'll talk to him about starting therapy again."

"Only if he wants to," Evan emphasized. "I don't want him to feel as if we think he's too fragile to handle a breakup." He narrowed his gaze at me. "Do you think he loved her?"

I shrugged. "She moved shortly after I even knew she existed. But you know how it is at that age. Everything seems so.... Major."

"Isn't that the truth?" Evan chuckled. "My first heartbreak felt like the end of the world."

"Exactly," I told him. "So, he's probably just going through normal teenage stuff." I hoped I was correct.

Finally, Evan nodded. "You're probably right. It sort of felt like two steps backward this week, and I got a little paranoid."

"I get it," I told him. "But he's going to be okay."

"Okay." He shrugged, looking somewhat relieved. "I'll go home tonight. I just want to see Michael one more time before I go."

I stifled a groan. Michael wouldn't be home for four more hours, and I didn't have time to babysit my ex. I had more important things on my plate, like finding a missing gnome and stopping a psycho sibling. On top of that, my anima-magic had been triggered, and I had no idea what disaster would follow once it was activated.

Keir walked back into the living room. I glanced at him, and he gave me a slight headshake. Damn it. No Linda.

I could feel my blood pressure rising by the second. "Evan..." Bob jumped into my lap and began to purr.

"Where did he come fr-*ah-ah-chh*." Evan sneezed. "You know I'm *ah-ah-chhh*. Allergic."

"Then I guess it's a good thing you don't live here," I told him, "Because I have a cat now. You remember Bob."

Evan sneezed a couple more times as he backed away from me. "I can't stay here with that cat."

"Aww." I made a pouty face as I gave Bob a grateful scritch between the ears. "That's too bad. I was so looking forward to catching up."

"Har har." He sneezed again. "How much dander does that cat have?"

Just enough, apparently. Evan hadn't been sneezing before Bob showed up, even though Bob spent a lot of time in the house. It stood to reason that his dander would be everywhere, yet Evan only reacted when Bob was in the room. All this led me to believe that my chonky-chonky-cuddle-monkey was messing with my ex.

"You better wait for Michael back at your motel."

"I gave up my room," Evan complained. "I don't have anywhere to go."

"I'm sure you'll find something to keep you busy. Call a friend. Go have lunch. Go shopping." I was okay with anything that would take him anywhere else but here. "I don't care what you do. Just go."

Evan looked shocked. "I thought we were past all this."

"All what?" Bob began to purr aggressively louder.

I felt Keir's hand on my shoulder. To Evan, he said, "You should leave."

"Stay out of this," Evan told him. "This is between Iris and me."

Keir's fingers tensed. I reached back and cupped his hand before he could react, then I narrowed my gaze at Evan. "There's nothing between us anymore. If you have something more to say about Michael, I'll listen, but otherwise, I need you to leave."

He peered at me as if I'd grown a third nostril. "When did you become so bitter?"

"Seriously?" I let out a weighted breath and shook my head. "Go to Hell, Evan."

The room darkened, and the air warmed. A faint corona of light rose from the hardwood floor under Evan's feet.

He wobbled in place. "What's happening?" His tone was a mix of fear and confusion.

I set Bob aside and got to my feet. Keir was around the couch and heading toward Evan.

The circle of light widened. Inside the ring was a bright, patterned line with three protrusions. "Move," I yelled to Evan. "Get out of the circle."

The light made him look almost ghostly, especially when his mouth dropped open and a loud, horrific cry filled the room. The illumination exploded into a blinding light, and when it fell away, Evan was gone.

Adrenaline dried my mouth, my throat, and my eyes. I swallowed hard, blinking rapidly as I tried to wrap my brain around what had just happened.

I pivoted my gaze to Keir. He had moved to the spot where the radiant circle had appeared and gobbled my ex up.

When I found my voice, I asked him, "What did I do?"

CHAPTER 2

I STARED IN HORROR AT WHERE THE SHINING CIRCLE had appeared as the ramifications set in. One minute I'd fantasized about Evan getting swallowed up by the floor, and then, like a completely irresponsible bonehead, I'd said the words that had made it happen. "I've sent my husband to Hell."

"Ex," Keir amended.

I gave him a flat look. "You know what I mean." Maybe the archdruids had been right to consider binding my powers. Evan wouldn't be paying the price for my erratic, spontaneous magic if they had.

"I do know what you mean," he told me. "But I don't think this was you."

"Clearly, it is." I gesticulated emphatically at the place where Evan had stood. "I told him to go to Hell, and to Hell, he went."

Keir put his hands on my shoulders in a reassuring way. "It doesn't work like that, Iris."

I didn't feel reassured. "Then tell me how it works

because there hasn't been a rule book regarding my magic so far. It's unpredictable and even more dangerous when I'm stressed or angry. How can you be sure this wasn't my fault?"

"The circle isn't something you can just conjure out of nowhere."

Keir rubbed his jawline with the back of his knuckles as he studied the floor in front of us. "I think the most important thing to focus on right now is how to get him back."

I arched a brow. "Definitely need to get him back. Michael will be home from school in a few hours, and he'll have questions if his dad isn't here. Oh, God." I staggered back until my legs hit the couch. "How am I going to face Michael?" I sat down. "I wish Linda was here." I glanced over to the kitchen arch. "No sign of her?"

Keir shook his head. "No sign of her."

I sat down, put my head between my knees, and sucked in a terrified breath.

Keir rubbed my back. "The circle on the ground. I didn't get a good look at it, but I'm pretty sure it was a Hecate wheel. I saw what looked like three spokes, but it happened so fast I can't be certain."

"A heck-a-what?"

He stood to his full height. "It's technically called a strophalos, but most witches would recognize it as a symbol for the Triple Goddess. The fact that you don't know what a Hecate wheel is tells me this isn't your magic."

Hecate wheel, strophalos, Triple Goddess, and all the other mumbo jumbo wouldn't make a difference to my ex-husband. He was gone. Disappeared from my living room in a flash of blinding light. "I'm not sure that's going to make a difference in the grand scheme of things. Michael isn't going to care if it was my powers or someone else's that took his dad." At least, I hoped he was taken. The alternative that he had been vaporized was too horrible to even consider.

"If he's alive, we'll get him back."

"I can't think about the ifs." I wrapped my arms across my chest. "Getting Evan back is my number one priority."

Keir nodded. "We'll get him back." He retrieved his phone from his jeans.

"Who are you calling?"

"Reinforcements."

Reinforcements turned out to be his sister Luanne, my sister Marigold, and the ifrit Zev. Keir hadn't told them about Evan, only that we needed them. They'd dropped everything and hauled their butts to my house without question.

Marigold, who was a head taller than she used to be now that the goddess Macha had transformed her into a giantess hybrid, almost had to duck as she entered the front door. Zev, who had lost his fire, also thanks to the goddess, was now a head taller as well so that they were evenly matched in size. They made goo-goo eyes at each other like newlyweds, and I was about to blow their bliss all to shit.

On the other hand, Luanne was decked out in her black tactical gear, her hair pulled back in a severe pony, and she looked like she was all business and no play.

"Oh, Iris," my sister said with heartfelt sympathy. She

swept across the room and rested her hands on my shoulders. "What's happened? Is it Linda? Did you find out anything?"

I shook my head. "It's Evan."

Her worried expression turned to a scowl. "What did that bastard do? I'll kill him."

"He didn't do anything to me," I told her. "It's what I've potentially done to him."

"If you killed him, no one would fault you."

"Michael would fault me. Adam too."

Marigold sucked her teeth. "Adam can kiss my heinie."

"Hey," Zev complained. "Only I am allowed to kiss your heinie."

She blushed, but I could tell she was pleased. It was cute, but now was not the time for cute.

"A glowing circle showed up and ate my ex-husband."

Zev looked to Keir. He nodded his confirmation. "A strophalos," he added.

"Someone invoked the triple goddess. Powerful magic," Lu said. "Not tru-craft, though."

"That's what I thought," Keir affirmed. "That's why I don't think Iris had anything to do with it grabbing Evan."

"Not tru-craft?" I asked. "How can you know?"

Keir shrugged. "Because tru-craft doesn't require the summoning of a goddess to work."

"But isn't that exactly what I did when I channeled Macha to take on that snotty monster when it attacked Iron Grove?"

He shook his head. "It's not the same thing. You can't just summon a goddess circle to disappear someone."

"In my defense, I didn't summon the goddess," I clarified. "She hijacked my body without my permission."

"And thankfully, she did. She saved Zev and me from turning into a pile of goo," Marigold said.

I nodded at my sister. "And I'm grateful, but none of this gets me closer to finding Evan, and Michael will be home in..." I glanced at the clock on my DVR. It was almost one o'clock. "He'll be home in three hours." My frustration was at an eight. "Why did Evan have to come here? If he'd stayed away, I wouldn't be dealing with this shit on top of all the other shit I'm dealing with."

"As much as I hate Evan for what he did to you, I don't think any of this is his fault," Marigold said. "Show us where it happened."

Keir took the lead and pointed out the place on the floor where the illuminated wheel had appeared. Lu and Zev smartly took a step back, but Marigold leaned in for a closer look. "I don't see anything. No scorch marks or any sign of it." She glanced at Keir. "Is that normal?"

"I think we need to consult a witch," Lu suggested.

"Iris is a witch," Marigold said.

"Iris is tru-craft by birthright. Her powers are manifestations of her magical destiny. It's not something she had to study or work for," Lu explained.

"Hey," I complained. "I work." I had all the minor concussions from my lessons with Linda to prove it.

Lu waved me off. "You know what I mean. We need a witch who has been studying the craft longer than four months and knows symbology."

Once I got past my bruised pride, it struck me that we

knew a witch—an eclectic witch who also happened to be my water guardian. "We should call Carver."

"Good idea," Keir agreed.

Lu looked skeptical. "He has ties to Thomas."

Thomas was Carver's biological father, and that was enough for her. The woman had a deep loathing for Thomas. Lu blamed him for her grandfather's death. I didn't have the same antagonistic relationship with the old tru-crafter, but I didn't trust him right now. He was my friend, but that didn't supersede his complete loyalty to Freya, Iron Grove's archdruid. He was tied to her in the same way that Keir was tied to me. If my interests overlapped with Freya's, Thomas would always choose her side. Unfortunately, after the past four days, I didn't trust Freya or any of the archdruids as far as I could throw them.

But Carver was my guardian. He wouldn't betray me. At least, I hoped he wouldn't. I got up and dug my phone from my purse. "I'm calling him."

"Bad idea," Lu warned.

"I thought we liked Carver," Marigold asked.

"He's cool," Lu replied. "But I don't know if I trust him to not go running to daddy the moment that he thinks Iris is out of control again."

I glared at her. "Hey, now. I don't plan to lose control."

Lu smirked. "You never do."

"If you're not going to be helpful, you can go," Keir told his sister sharply.

She lifted her hands, arms bending at the elbows in mock surrender. "Okay, touchy."

"Hi, Carver," Marigold chirped. She held her phone

out to the room, speaker on. "What do you know about Hecate Wheels?"

"Hello, Marigold and everyone else." Carver had black hair, dark eyes, a hawkish nose, and bushy brows like his father. He grinned at us through the screen.

"You have his phone number?" I asked, putting my phone back in my purse.

She gave me a crooked smile. "We exchanged digits at the grove."

"Did you now?" Zev asked.

"Jealous?" Marigold's gaze softened. "Don't be. We're friends."

"As fun as this conversation is," Carver said, "I'm in the middle of a job, so we need to make this quick. What do you want to know about the Strophalos of Hecate?"

"Can one just randomly appear and wheel-nap cheating ex-husbands?" I asked.

Carver's brow quirked up. "That happened?"

I nodded. "Right in the middle of my living room."

He pursed his lips in thought. "Someone would have to invoke the circle. It wouldn't just appear without a catalyst."

"So...not me?"

He chuckled. "Doubtful. Do you know of Hecate?"

I gave him a bland look. "Not really. I've heard the name before, probably on television, but that's about it. Keir called her the triple goddess." I wasn't sure what that meant, but it sounded like three times the trouble.

"She's sometimes known as the triple goddess because it is believed that she goes through cycles from the maiden to the mother to the crone."

"Of course, those are the only cycles women can exist in," Lu muttered.

I didn't disagree with her irritation. In past eras, a woman my age would fall into the crone stage. Screw that noise.

Carver either didn't hear her or ignored the comment as he continued. "Others believe Hecate is three different goddesses who work together as a powerful unit to overcome their foes. They are believed to control the moon and the sun and have power over life and death."

Better than maiden, mother, and crone, but not by much. "None of this is making me feel better." To be frank, I was freaking the freakout.

"She's also the goddess of magic and spells." A crackle and hiss sounded over the speaker. Carver's eyes darted to the left.

"Do you need to go?" I asked.

"I have a few minutes," he replied. "But that's about it."

I leaned toward the screen as if I could peer around him. "What are you doing, exactly?"

"I can tell you what I'm doing *ooooorrrrr*...I can answer your questions." He arched a brow, then quickly said, "But I don't have time for both."

"Fine." I nodded for him to go ahead. "Magic and spells. What else?"

"She's been accused of being an agent for darkness, but most consider her deeds are proof of her powers being for the light."

"Wait." I put my finger up. "Like Fade and Bright?" My powers came from both places, and from what I had learned over the past several months, that was rare indeed. Bright was the ability to create and change something and make it new. Fade was the opposite. It allowed me to destroy things that already existed to harness the object's metaphysical energy.

Carver's dark eyes brightened. "Exactly like Fade and Bright. Neither is good or bad. Both types of magic can be used for good or ill. The triple goddess is much the same. It's about the practitioner, not the origin of the magic."

This might have been a fascinating lesson if I hadn't been worried about where my ex was. But I needed to know less about Hecate's history and more about who might have used her magic to snatch Evan. "Can't the goddess be all like," I waved my hands on either side of my head, "stealing someone's ex isn't cool, and just deny the person who cast the spell?"

The eclectic witch chuckled and shook his head. "It doesn't work like that. It's not the actual goddess who would've done the abduction. It would have been the magic she gifts to her follower. I've never heard of the ability to locate and translocate a human being through the wheel. It would take someone with some extreme ability."

I grimaced. "Like a sorcerer with a vendetta?"

There was another hiss behind Carver and a bright flare to the left of him. He winced, but he didn't hang up. "You think Bogmall did this?"

"I don't know what to think." I shook my head. "Why in the world would she target my ex? Keir and I were in the room with Evan. If it was Bogmall, I think she would have cast her net on a bigger fish."

A crackle followed by a loud bang made Carver jump. "I have to go, Iris. I'll look into your mystery when I'm done here and see what I can find. I'm afraid I don't have any easy answers for you." Another bang and flash.

"Go," I said, "Before whatever you're doing gets out of hand."

His eyes widened. "Too late for that." On that note, he ended the call.

I handed Marigold back her phone. "Well, that was a big ol' waste of time."

"We'll figure it out," Keir said in a soothing voice that made me want to punch something.

I gave him a flat look. "I love you, but I need more urgent panic and less laid-back calm."

The corner of his mouth quirked into a half smile. "I'll let you handle the urgent panic."

"The only thing I urgently want to handle right now is my bladder. It was a long trip." I grabbed my purse. "Be right back."

Even if I hadn't had to pee, I had needed a moment to reset my brain. The past few days of chaos, including the glowing circle nabbing my ex-husband, had fried my cylinders. I desperately needed a couple of minutes to get my head on right.

I sat down on the toilet and retrieved my phone from my purse. Mindlessly, I searched scenes for hidden objects on a game app I hadn't played in a long time. It forced me to think about something other than the chaos that was my life.

My phone tinkled, and a message popped up on the screen. The call was from an Anonymous number. It said, *Do you want him back?* There was an image that showed up under the message. It was Evan. His cheek was bruised, his lip was split, and there was a gash over his wide, frightened eyes.

Who is this?

Call me and find out. But tell anyone, and I'll gut him like a pig. Oink. Oink.

Great. This was officially a kidnapping, and I was about to get a ransom demand.

Well, shit.

CHAPTER 3

I YANKED MY PANTS UP BECAUSE THERE WAS NO WAY IN hell I would call whoever had Evan with my underwear at my knees. Automatically, I grabbed the bottle of talcum powder from the second drawer in my vanity, cranked the top a half turn, and squeezed a small amount into my hand.

"Beyond these walls, no sound to hear. Within these walls, my words are clear." I smacked my hands together, scattering the dust around the small room. Now, none of the supernaturals in my living room would hear the call I was about to make. One good thing about the text, Evan was alive. Or at least he'd been when they shot me the message thirty seconds ago. And another good thing, my magic hadn't been responsible for his disappearance. Not exactly a victory, but the revelation helped me to let go of some of my anxiety so I could focus on what I had to do next to get him back.

I tapped the callback icon on the text message and

waited for some asshole to pick up. I didn't have to wait long.

"Are you alone?" the strange voice asked. I'd watched enough thrillers to recognize a voice modifier when I heard it.

"Why Evan?"

"I'll ask the questions," the voice said, evident irritation in its tone.

I should've been scared and worried. Instead, I was pissed. I hung up.

The phone rang. I ignored it.

A text popped up on the screen. *Call now, or he dies.*

Why? He has nothing to do with the world of magic. Why him?

There were three dots, then nothing. Why were they acting coy?

Finally, the words, *answer the call*, popped up.

The phone rang. I answered. "I swear if you shitheads harm one curly hair on his head, I'll—"

"You're not in a position to make threats, Ms. Everlee."

Ms. Everlee, huh? Maybe this wasn't Bogmall. I wasn't sure if that made me feel better or worse.

The next words from the kidnapper sent ice water through my veins. "Besides, it wasn't his curly hair that we wanted."

"Not his curly hair...."

"How could we know there were two people in your home with such pretty blond locks? But don't worry. We have more samples to choose from. Your place was a bounty of DNA for our spells."

Shit. My gut dropped, and I felt lightheaded. They'd been trying to trap Michael. Evan had been an accidental get. And from what they were saying, they were willing to keep trying until they got the right Callahan. My jaw flexed as fear burned my throat. "Leave Michael out of this. Just tell me what you want."

"Better," the voice said. "Come to Grave Hall at midnight. There is a cabin off double A road about a mile down on the left."

"Release Evan," I countered. "You don't need him. Not if your threat is real."

"That's a fair point, Ms. Everlee, but how can I be sure you'll keep your end of the bargain?"

"Because I want you to leave Michael out of this, and the only way that happens is if I do what you say, right?"

There were three clicks then the voice answered, "We accept your terms, but if you don't show up and show up alone, we will have a spell ready to take your son, and we won't worry about the shape he's in when he gets to us." Another click ended the call.

Shit, shit, shit. Whoever took Evan had been in my house. They'd taken hair samples, thinking it was Michael, and had accidentally grabbed Evan by mistake. Now they wanted me to meet them at Grave Hall. It was only about twenty miles from Southill Village, but the area was higher on the mountain, and this time of year, it was heavy with fog and clouds. It was going to take me at least an hour to drive it. How in the heck was I going to get away from here without alerting anyone? Was it wise to go without any backup? No, absolutely not. Did I believe they could follow through on their threat to

Michael if provoked? Yes, I did. Still, it wouldn't be easy. I was a terrible liar, so it was best to avoid elaborate stories. I had time to worry and make a plan. Midnight was still ten hours away.

What did these people want from me? The voice had said "we," but that didn't tell me anything except there was more than one of them. For all I knew, they weren't even human. It could be a tribe of angry ogres or vengeful giants. I'd taken on every challenge that had come my way, and I'd won. This would be the first time I was utterly alone. The idea was terrifying. The goal was to burn the motherfuckers to the ground, along with all their spelling supplies connected to Michael's DNA. Since I couldn't be sure it would work, I'd leave a note in case I didn't make it back.

With my mind made up, I canceled the silence spell. After, I washed the powder off my hands and dried them. I wanted nothing more than to immediately tell Keir everything. "Michael," I reminded myself. "I'm a mother first."

A knock startled me from my panicked thoughts. "Hey, babe. You okay in there?"

"Fine," I lied. "Coming out now."

"We have a situation," Keir said.

I opened the door. "Worse than the current situation?"

Keir made a face that I couldn't decipher. "Not worse, but definitely going to need some diplomacy."

"Iris!" I heard Evan yell. "What in the hell is going on around here?"

My eyes widened. "He's back?"

"Showed up about ten seconds ago in the same place he'd disappeared."

The mysterious voice had kept their part of the bargain. Evan was back. Of course, I was left with the fallout of explaining. What a mess.

"Iris!" I could hear his footfalls in the hallway. He was heading to my bedroom.

Hell, no. "I'll be out in a minute," I said sharply. "Do *not* come in here."

I heard him stop. "I want to know why I disappeared from your living room, wound up in a dark room where someone tied me up and beat the crap out of my face, Iris. What are you into? Is Michael safe? I want an explanation, and I want it now."

"Give me a damn minute, Evan. I'll explain everything." Well, as much of everything that would make sense to him. Maybe his experience could give me a heads-up about what I was walking into tonight.

I leaned into Keir, resting my cheek against his shoulder. I sagged with relief when his arms wrapped around me.

He stroked my hair. "We'll get through this."

"Thank you for saying we."

"Always," he replied. "You ready?"

"Nope." I patted his chest, straightened my back, and pulled up my shoulders. "But let's do it anyway."

I heaved a heavy sigh, mentally preparing myself, as I opened the door. I winced at the cuts and bruises on Evan's face.

He stared at me with narrowed eyes, his arms crossed tightly over his chest. "Tell me what's going on, or I'm going to the police."

I was surprised that hadn't been his first move.

Keir dipped his lips to my ear. "He can't find his phone."

"Ah." Whoever took him must've taken it. "I'm going to explain," I said. "But I'm going to need you to keep an open mind. But not in my bedroom." I shooed him away from my door. "Living room."

"Not if my life depended on it," he said.

Oh, yeah. He'd been eaten by the living room floor. "My bad. Outside to the garden?" I made it a question.

He glanced around at the walls, ceiling, and floor before glancing back at me. "Outside sounds like a plan." Evan turned on his heel and headed down the hall into the kitchen.

"He's calmer than I expected." I walked back into my room and grabbed my suitcase from the floor. I hoisted it onto the bed.

Keir arched his brow at me.

"Grimoire," I explained. "A little show and tell."

"What are you going to say to him?"

"I don't know." I sighed. "I'll make it up as I go along."

I asked the others to wait inside while I talked to Evan. The reason was two-fold. First, I thought an audience would make it harder for Evan to process that magic was real. Second, it would allow me to find out information about the people holding him since I planned to sneak off tonight to meet with them.

It was a mild mid-September, and the pink flowering kale and late-blooming purple and yellow pansies splashed the garden with color. My heart squeezed when I saw Evan sitting on the bench at the back of my yard, but no Linda. This was her domain, and for a second, I expected to see her stern, disapproving expression.

Evan interpreted my disappointment as a slight. He pointed to his bruised and battered face. "Explain this, please."

"It looks painful." I clasped my grimoire securely to my chest like a shield and sat next to him. "We should put some ice on it before it swells more."

"That's not an explanation." His brows knitted together. "I want to know why the hell I was standing in your living room one moment and tied to a chair by five monks the next."

"You were being held by monks? What did they look like?"

"They wore robes with hoods, so I couldn't see their faces." He rubbed his jaw. "But one of them packed a wallop."

I noticed a cut near his lip that looked like the start of a zigzag. "What did you get hit with?"

"A fist," Evan said. "He wore a big ass ring."

"Did it have some kind of design on it?" I asked hopefully. An insignia would be a clue.

Evan shook his head. "I felt it but didn't see it."

"And you're sure it was a man?"

"I can't be positive, but the fist was thick, and the knuckles hairy. That doesn't necessarily mean it wasn't a woman, but it makes it less likely." Evan stood up. "But that still doesn't explain what happened to me." He scrubbed his face with his palms, then turned his stark gaze on me. "What happened to me, Iris? No bullshit."

"Magic," I told him. "No bullshit."

CHAPTER 4

"You don't have to gaslight me, Iris. Tell me the truth. I can take it," Evan said. The way he was pacing and wringing his hands, I wasn't sure it was true.

I placed my grimoire on my lap and then patted the space next to me. "You're going to want to sit down for this."

He looked as if he wanted to argue, but after what looked like an epic internal debate, he gave me a curt nod and took a seat. "What's that?" He pointed to the tome of magic.

"It's the beginning." I shook my head. "At least, it's my beginning."

Evan reached out as if to touch the cover, but he stopped just short of contact. His hand hovered above the symbols. "It's an old book. Is it about your birth family?" His curiosity was piqued. "Did you find your biological mother?"

"Yes and no," I answered. "No, I didn't find my mother, but the book does contain my history, sort of." I flipped the cover open, exposing the handwritten list of names and dates. "Apparently, I come from a long line of women who possessed a kind of magic called tru-craft."

"You know how nuts you sound, right?"

I snorted. "You're telling me. When my power first started to develop, I thought I'd been drugged, and I was living in a psychedelic fog." I'd had my brother Rowan, an emergency department doctor, do a blood test. He hadn't found drugs, but the chemical composition of my blood had been entirely out of whack. "Instead, it was my magic sparking to life."

He gave me a pitying stare. "Iris, are you in trouble? Did you borrow money from the wrong person? You don't have to make up a fantastical story. We might not be together anymore, but that doesn't mean I stopped caring about you. You can trust me."

I let out an exasperated sigh. "I need you to listen to me."

"I am listening," he said.

"But you're not hearing." I leaned over and picked up a pink and white marbled stone about the size of my palm. I offered it to Evan.

He took it. "What's this for?"

I twirled my finger at the rock. "Take a good look at it and tell me what you see."

"It's Ozarkite." He turned it over in his hand. "Fairly common. Is it...magical?"

I snorted a laugh. "No. It's just a rock." I half-smiled and took it back from him. Holding the rock with my left hand, I positioned it between my thumb and forefinger. With my right index finger, I pressed the tip against the flat side of the rock. I closed my eyes and concentrated on the vibrational energy emanating from the Ozarkite. I manipulated my own energy to match the resonance and slid my finger straight through the surface and out the other end. "Ta-dah," I said quietly and wiggled my fingertip at him.

"How did you do that? Is that a trick? Some kind of illusion?"

I slid my finger out. "It's terra-craft. Earth magic." I gave him the rock back. "See for yourself."

He examined it a lot closer this time, then shook his head. "Show me something else."

"Fine. Here's another element." I held up my hand and lit my fingers on fire. "This is ignis-craft."

Evan blanched. "Does it burn?"

I shook my head. "Not my own fire." I shook my hand, and the flames went out.

"That'll come in handy if you ever decide to take up smoking." He chuckled, then winced and touched his fat lip. He still looked skeptical but was willing to go with it. "So, walk me through this, finishing with why those guys took me."

"I am a witch, for better or worse, and there are people and creatures out in the world who want the power that I have inside me. I think whoever took you is another one of these assholes in a long line of assholes. It's as simple and as complicated as that."

"Creatures? As in...what?"

"Well, there was a rock troll, a gargoyle, a fire god, a red cap disguised as dozens of leprechauns, a snotgurgle—"

He scoffed and rolled his eyes. "That's not a real thing."

I shivered as I remembered the horrifying slimy creature with its face-melting mucus. "Unfortunately, it's all too real."

The silence between us was long. He was trying his best.

"How did you get the book?"

"It's a grimoire." I stroked the vellum page, listing the women in my family that came before me. "It found me. Sort of. It belonged to my ancestors. When I touched it, it triggered the spark in me." Not completely accurate, but close enough for this conversation. "As to why those men, or whatever they are, took you, my best guess is that they were trying to get to me."

"They don't know you very well, then."

"What's that supposed to mean?"

"Only that, if they were trying to manipulate you into doing something, kidnapping me seems like a pretty lame way of going about it. It doesn't take a genius to figure out that you hate me."

I closed the grimoire and let out an irritated sigh. "I don't hate you, Evan. Not anymore. And just because I'm not in love with you or even like you much at this point doesn't mean I wouldn't care if you were kidnapped and beaten or worse. You're Michael's father. For better or worse, that connects us."

He eyed me suspiciously. "How did you get them to release me?"

"I did nothing," I lied.

"Iris, we might not be married anymore or even

friends, but I spent over twenty years with you. I know when you are holding something back."

I shot to my feet, clasping the grimoire against my chest. "That's rich coming from you. If only I could've read you as accurately as you seem to be able to read me."

Evan held up his hands. "I get it. I'm sorry. I don't have a right—"

"Damn straight, you don't have a right. The best thing you can do for yourself and for me is to leave town."

"For good?" He looked upset and confused. "My son is still here."

"Not for good." I glared at him, wishing he would just freaking go. I was sick of looking at his battered face, and I had a lot bigger problems than Evan to worry about. He was safe, and if he left town, he'd probably stay safe. "I just can't deal with you right now. It's better if you weren't here. There is stuff happening. Magic stuff. And you will only get in the way of me doing what I need to do to save myself and everyone I care about."

His brow dipped. "This is about Michael, isn't it?" His eyes widened. "You think they were after Michael and accidentally got me."

Jesus, my ex wasn't stupid. I hoped he was lying about my tells. "No, that's not what I think." A technical truth. I knew they'd been after Michael and not Evan.

"I'm not leaving town without our son. This whole situation is a mess, Iris. How could you mix Michael up in all this hoodoo-whacka-doo supernatural crap? You're supposed to protect him."

The hairs on the back of my neck raised. His accusations simultaneously fed into my guilt and my rage. I dropped the grimoire to the ground and focused all those negative feelings on something other than killing my ex-husband. I heard the cracking of stone before I saw my precious stone bench shatter and turn to dust under Evan's ass. The wind spun around my head as I concentrated on the particles of concrete. The pieces floated around Evan like a moving cage.

"Iris, stop," he demanded. The stone cage shrank. His demand became a plea. "Iris! Stop!"

"Iris!" I heard Keir call from behind me. "This won't solve anything."

I let out a scream of frustration, and the wall came down. I jabbed my finger at my chest. "I protect my son. I keep him safe. What do you do? Hurt him. Over and over. But I'm the bad guy? You wanted out of this family. Guess what? You're out."

Evan's voice was shaky as he got up from the ground. He stared at me as if I were a monster. "I never wanted out of the family, Iris. Just out of the marriage. Michael is my son too, and I love him. I will fight you for him if I have to."

"Dad," Michael said from the garden gate. He'd come home early. "I won't go with you. My home is here with Mom."

How long had he been on the other side? Had he heard our conversation? Shame replaced my anger. "Michael, it's okay," I said. "Go inside. We'll talk in a minute."

"No." His determined defiance made him seem more grown up. At seventeen, he wasn't as easy to boss around. "This is my problem as much as it is yours."

"Michael—"

He cut me off when he got close enough to see his dad's face. His blue eyes went wide. "Did you do this to him?"

"No," Evan and I both said simultaneously.

Evan shuffled nervously. "I walked into a wall."

"Bull shit." Michael closed the distance between us. "Someone used you as a punching bag."

"It's okay," I told Evan. "Michael knows about me. He knows everything."

"Let him come home with me," Evan implored. "If only until you get your...stuff sorted. He'll be safer with me."

"He won't." I shook my head. "If the bad guys want him, they're going to be able to get him no matter where he is. At least if he's with me, I have a shot at stopping them."

"What bad guys?" Michael asked.

I looked at my nearly adult kid and shrugged. "I wish I knew. Maybe Bogmall, maybe someone else, maybe a monster."

Was Evan right? Was I failing my child? I felt like the crappiest mother in the world. Maybe he would be safer in St. Louis. All I had was the word of a kidnapper that he had Michael's DNA and that if I didn't do as he said, he'd keep trying his spell until he got my boy. I planned on caving to the kidnappers' demands. Maybe that would take Michael completely out of the mix.

I looked at Michael. "Maybe you should go stay with your dad for a couple of days."

"I'm not leaving you." His jaw flexed. "Whatever is happening, I won't leave. We're in this together."

My heart jumped. I put my arms around Michael and hugged him as if it were the last time. "You can't help this time," I told him. "And I might not be able to do what I have to do if I'm worrying about you."

"I'm not leaving," he said when I let him go. He turned to his dad. "Go back to St. Louis. I'll come up in a few weeks for a visit."

"Michael, I can't let you stay behind. Not with the dangers surrounding your mother." He gave our son a beseeching look. "Please, I just want to protect you."

"I'm protected here," Michael said. Marigold, Luanne, and Zev walked out into the garden from the kitchen and stood next to Keir at my back. Michael blinked his surprise when he saw how his aunt had grown in size, but he recovered quickly. He jerked his thumb at them. "They'll watch over me."

Bob rubbed his fat body against my calves. Fair Konig zipped out of a bush and vowed, in his heavy accent, "As Iris Everlee has kept my children safe, I vow the pixie folk will do the same for hers. Wherever he is, we will have eyes on him. He will never be alone. Not for a second. This is our pledge."

I gave Fair Konig a grateful look.

Michael, however, blanched. "The bathroom is a no-pixie zone. Just saying."

Evan's face paled. He looked like he was about to puke. "What...who..." He shook his head in disbelief at the flying pixie. "Never mind," he blustered. "You win, Iris. I'll go. But only as far as the Village Motel. I won't leave until I know Michael is okay. He is my concern, whether you like it or not."

"Evan," I said. "Don't tell anyone, okay?"

He gave me a look of pure incredulity and scoffed. "Who in the world would believe me?"

"Fair point."

"I'll walk you out, Dad," Michael said.

As they left the backyard, I felt Keir's arms as he wrapped them around me. I sank back into the warmth of his body and turned my face until my cheek pressed against his chest. I could hear his heart beating, and the calm, steady rhythm soothed me.

"Do you think I should've made him go?"

"I think he's old enough to do what he's going to do. If you sent him away, he'd find a way to come back. He loves you, Iris. It's something we all have in common."

I manufactured a smile that I didn't feel. "We have to find Linda. I can't do this without her."

"We'll find her," Keir said. "And we'll stop anybody who comes for you or Michael."

"It's what we do."

"Damn straight," Lu agreed. "These jerks are going to wish they'd messed with a different witch and her coven when this is over. We'll make them pay."

Marigold put a hand on my back. "No one messes with my sister and gets away with it."

"See," Keir dipped his head and kissed my shoulder. "Now, let's go inside. Zev thinks he might know how to find Linda, but it's going to take some finesse."

CHAPTER 5

With Evan gone, I wanted to hear more about Marigold and Zev's plan to find Linda. Their idea sounded farfetched, but I lived in Farfetched these days, so I tried to keep an open mind.

"You want to talk to a badger?" I asked.

"Not any specific badger," Zev said. "Any badger on the mountain will do." I noticed that his eyes were a dark honey color now that he no longer had his fire. What was an ifrit without fire? For Zev, the answer was happy. He had a carefree air about him that I'd never seen him possess.

Marigold, also in the happy category, nodded enthusiastically. "I can talk to animals now."

"You can?"

"I might be descended from woodland giants. They have that ability." She beamed a smile at me. "I tested it out on a squirrel, and while I'll admit the damn thing talked almost too fast to understand, I was able to make out that she wanted me the hell away from her tree. So, then I talked to a raccoon, and that sucker told me that badgers have a special friendship with the gnomes and that if anyone would know where the wee folk lived, they would." She spoke with great enthusiasm. "So you see, if we can find a badger, we can find Linda or at least Linda's donsy."

A donsy was a community of gnomes, and they hoped that Linda's husband might know where she was, and if he didn't, he might be able to help us locate her. Gnomes were solitary creatures, and Linda and her husband didn't spend much time together. It was their way, and it worked. They had been married for over a hundred years. But it also meant, if she hadn't gone home to him, chances were good Morlan had no idea she was missing.

The idea was sound, except I needed clarity on the animal talking part. "And who gave you the idea to talk to animals?"

Marigold's smile faltered. "Don't be mad."

"Why would I be mad?"

"Because I know you're angry with him...."

"Thomas," I said.

She nodded. "I'd asked him about my transformation before we left Iron Grove. He did some kind of magic test on me and said he thought I belonged to the wood-land giants, which I told you. But that gave him an idea about finding Linda. According to Thomas, gnomes and animals are allies. They have very close relationships and live in harmony with each other."

It was hard to imagine Linda living in harmony with anyone. Regardless, I didn't like who the information came from. "And how did Thomas know about Linda?"

She flushed. "I told him that too." Her expression registered dismay. "Thomas is on our side."

"He's on Iron Grove's side. He's on the archdruids' side."

"Only Freya," she countered. "He's fine with the rest of the arch-idiots rotting in their own sewage." She shrugged. "His words, not mine. Besides, what could it hurt if Freya knew about Linda being missing?"

"So after you talked to Thomas, you found a squirrel and a raccoon hanging around at Iron Grove for you to speak to? Convenient, don't you think?"

Luanne snorted. "I'd say." She couldn't be objective when it came to Thomas since she blamed him for her grandfather's death.

Marigold straightened her skirt. "The squirrel was in a tree at my house when we got home this morning, and the raccoon had gotten caught in my garbage can. He was grateful that I'd let him out, which made him all too happy to share the information about the badgers," she huffed.

Zev, Keir, and Luanne smartly stayed out of the conversation.

I was desperate to find Linda—desperate enough to try the animal grapevine. The gnome had been gone less than a day, but her condition when we'd rescued her made me fear the worst. "Okay. You guys find a badger and see if they can help find Morlan and the other gnomes."

Zev stood up and held his hand out to Marigold. "Come, *ātashé del-am*. We shall search for the badger and find the little earth guardian."

Marigold smiled coyly as she got up from the chair.

She turned her gaze to me. "I'll do everything I can to get her back for you."

I nodded. "Thank you." I didn't hold out much hope for their success, but at least they were doing something. It was more than I could say for myself. I had to figure out a way to leave the house tonight without Keir or Michael noticing, drive an hour to Grave Hall to meet with my son's would-be kidnappers. They said they'd had a spell ready to take him the minute they felt betrayed. I loved Linda, but there was a possibility she was safe with her family and trying to mend her broken parts. If I didn't do what the asshole on the phone wanted, Michael would definitely be in danger. I couldn't allow that to happen.

"I'm exhausted," I said to Keir after the others left. "I'd like to be alone tonight to decompress. You don't mind, do you?"

"I don't like leaving you alone. Not with what happened to Evan. It could've been meant for you. You and Michael should come and stay with me."

"In your tiny home?" His place had a living room that doubled as a kitchen and a library, a small loft with a mattress, a bathroom that doubled as his closet, and a compost toilet. No, thank you. "I'll take my chances here."

"I'll sleep on the couch," he said.

"I'll be fine," I assured him. "Go home."

He gave me a suspicious look, and I wondered if Evan was right about me. Could Keir tell I was holding information back? For Michael's sake, I hoped not.

"I don't want to fight about it," I reiterated. "Just go. We'll talk tomorrow."

Keir stood up from the table. "Okay." He leaned over and gave me a kiss. "Tomorrow."

"Thank you." I felt bad for keeping the truth from him, but I'd told him before that Michael was my priority. I would always put my son first, no matter what. It didn't stop me from feeling like a totally bad person for lying to the guy who would always put me first. "Hey." I stood up and laced my fingers behind his neck. "I love you."

He smiled, soft and sad. "I love you too. I am here for you, Iris. There isn't anything I wouldn't do for you."

"I know." I kissed him, relishing the sizzle as our lips met. "I'll explain everything tomorrow."

He nodded. "I'll stay in town with Lu. That way, if you need me, you can reach me by cellphone." His place had no cell service of any kind, and while I had to go through with this plan alone, I was glad that if I did need to call him, I'd be able to reach him.

"Thank you."

LATER THAT EVENING, Michael was eyeball deep in a video game with two of the younger pixies hooting and cheering him on as he bounced a crash car all around the inside of a sphere. He was playing a team game with a couple of his buddies, and while the irony wasn't wasted on me, it made me feel better that he wasn't alone.

Meeting these men was a big undertaking, and I had my little Linda playing in my ear.

Stupid, Kleinkind. Going off to meet strange men who wield magic in the middle of the night only proves you are an ignoramus who has learned nothing over the past few months!

Even lost, she was mean and right. The only thing missing was a rock being thrown at my head. She'd also tell me that I needed to consult my grimoire. I had looked up anima or spirit as an element when we discovered that Bogmall had been using it to possess the cheerleader's mom. The craft involved the ability to divine the spirit world, read someone's past, present, and future, and —if the blonde hexen-bitch was an indication—an anima-craft witch could possess people. Bogmall had done it twice now in attempts to get at me.

Was there some kind of spell that I could come up with that would show me the outcome of the night? Wouldn't that be nice? As it was, while my anima-craft had been activated the previous night, it wasn't like I'd sparked to it. For the previous elements, it had taken days to weeks for them to spark to power, and two of the elements had been so wild they almost killed me. I shuddered to think what kind of havoc wild spirit magic would wreak on my body.

I set my grimoire on the kitchen table and made myself a nice cup of tea, then opened it up. Bob jumped up on the table and flopped down behind the book. I didn't know if that was a good sign or a bad one, but I forged ahead.

"Okay, Grim, what guidance do you have for me tonight? Am I doing the right thing by going it alone?"

Inked words began to appear on the slightly yellow page.

Blood of my blood, down a path you will fall.

Tears of my tears, you must heed the call.

Between life and death is the divine. To master spirit, you must walk a line.

Summon strength from both Fade and Bright, or you will lose yourself in the coming fight.

Goddess, help you.

I closed the grimoire and sighed. "Super helpful, Grim," I told it. "As always, thank you for the clarity." Did the ancient tome understand sarcasm? I hoped so. I'd asked it for a little guidance, and all it brought was more gloom and doom.

I decided an internet search would bring the clarity my grimoire lacked. I was wrong. I typed: *what do I do to open myself up to spirit magic?*

I discovered there were four hundred gazillion spiritual gurus on the world wide web who, for a fee, would guide me through a spiritual awakening. I was tempted to pull out my credit card, but I had strong doubts about the validity of their claims. Besides, I knew how to meditate. Before cross-fit, my sister Rose had gone through a yoga phase. She'd talked me into going to a couple of mindfulness classes with her until I discovered that sitting criss-cross applesauce in a hot, sweaty room with fifteen other people doing nothing but breathing wasn't a good time for me.

I closed my eyes and concentrated on opening my third eye, or whatever I needed to open, to spark my anima. From experience, I knew it was there somewhere inside me, burbling under the surface, waiting for the worst possible moment to rear its ugly head.

"Oooooooooh," I said slowly on a long exhalation,

then inhaled and repeated. "Ooooooooh." After a few minutes of meditation, I was nowhere closer to tapping into the energy. How in the world had Bogmall done it? Oh, yeah, right. She'd stolen it by killing a living tru-crafter. Frankly, her determination to gain power at any cost scared me.

I looked up: *how does someone possess someone else?*

There were a lot of articles on spirit possession, but unsurprisingly there was no step-by-step Wikihow on the subject. It frustrated me how good Bogmall was at magic. Of course, she'd known about it her whole life, so she'd probably understood it better than me. Cripes. Was she really my twin sister? I'd always heard that twins had a special bond. Even the ones separated at birth sometimes lived nearly parallel lives. With Bogmall, I hadn't felt a single connection to her during any of our encounters. Of course, we looked nothing alike, which meant we weren't identical twins, so even if we were biological twins, we didn't share the exact DNA. It didn't make me feel better. She wanted me dead. No amount of familial connection was going to change that.

My doorbell chimed. It was almost nine, and I didn't have time for company.

I looked out my living room curtain at the front porch and was surprised to see Carver. He rang the bell again as I opened the door.

"What are you doing here?" I asked.

"Hello to you, too, Iris." He looked past me to my living room. "I was commanded to come to you."

"Commanded? By who?"

He shrugged. "I'm not sure," he said. "I was in the

middle of a ritual cleansing for a client's new home, and a voice told me to drop everything and go to you."

I waved him inside. "Do you always listen to the random voice in your head?"

"Yes," he said. "The voice has guided me most of my life, and she's never been wrong."

"And what did this voice tell you to do once you got here?"

Carver scratched his beak-like nose and looked at me as if he were about to tell me that the dog ate his homework. "She told me that if you go alone, you will die."

Well, shit. I knew there was a possibility that the guys who took Evan planned to kill me, but I'd been banking on a fighting chance to thwart them.

I gestured to my kitchen table. "I guess you better sit down so we can talk."

CHAPTER 6

"YOU KNOW I'M AN ECLECTIC WITCH," CARVER TUCKED his messy, light brown hair behind his ears in a gesture of uncertainty. "It means I wasn't born with magic."

"That's not entirely true," I told him. "You're part tru-craft witch, part naiad and sylph. It might have taken a long time for your abilities to manifest, but I have a feeling they were always there. Kind of like mine."

"I won't argue with you about it because you're not wrong." He shook his head. "But until recently, I'd only done magic through ritual spells, symbology, rune work, and other types of witchcraft and alchemy that rely on tapping into nature and the universe."

"I'm following," I said. "But I'm not sure it's getting us closer to our destination. Where does the voice come in?"

"These types of magic only work through divine inter-vention, whether the divine is nature or a god or goddess."

I thought about Macha and the way she'd rode my body to victory against the snotgurgle. It had been her magic, through me, that had saved my sister Marigold. "So, you're saying this voice is one of those two things? Nature or a deity."

"Yes, and she has been guiding me for as long as I can remember, even before I understood what she was."

"Who is *she*?"

"Hecate," he answered.

I felt as if I'd had the wind knocked out of me. "As in Hecate of the Strophalos that swallowed my ex-husband from my living room and spat him out somewhere else?"

He nodded, his expression stark. "Yes, that Hecate."

My body warmed with anger. "How come you didn't say all this over the video call earlier?"

"Lots of people worship and pray to the goddess," he replied. "I told you she is neither an agent for good nor bad. Only the practitioner."

"I'm beginning to think the practitioner in front of me is pretty suspect." And I'd invited him into my home. My kid was just down the hall. No. Carver was my water guardian, right? I could trust him the way I trusted Linda, Zev, and Fair Konig. I wanted so badly to believe it. "You should've told me."

"Maybe you're right, but honestly, there are over a million witches in the world who follow Hecate. This isn't about her, not really, so I didn't think my affiliation mattered."

"Do all these million witches have her talking in their ear?"

He wrinkled his nose and rubbed his palms against his black jeans. "Probably not."

"How many have you met that did?"

"None."

"Then maybe you should've freaking told me that you had a direct line to Hecate when her wheel was used to kidnap someone from my house."

"I'm telling you now."

"When you were ordered to."

Carver's brows pinched together, causing deep creases between his eyes. "Because now it's relevant," he countered. "Whatever you believe, Iris, I wasn't trying to keep information from you. You knowing that I prayed to Hecate as part of my practice wouldn't have made a difference in the information I gave you. I'm tied to you for reasons beyond what I ever imagined, but that doesn't mean I have to share every aspect of my life with you. I'm still a person who had a whole life before I met you three days ago. You don't have that authority over me."

His words cut deep. Is that what I did? Fate brought Keir, Lu, Linda, Zev, Fair Konig, and now, Carver into my circle of existence. Did I take them for granted? Did I expect them to give me everything while I refused to do the same?

"You're right," I muttered. "I'm sorry."

Carver frowned. "I want to help you, Iris. I want your safety more than I should."

"I think that's part of the guardian gig," I said unhappily. "I'm sorry for that too. Please, tell me your message."

"If you go alone, you will die." He tapped the table. "That's pretty much the gist. Only, she was insistent that I tell you in person."

"Why?"

"Because I think she wants me to go with you."

"But you don't know where I'm going."

"No," he agreed. "But wherever it is, that's where I need to be."

I got up and carried my teacup to the sink. "You can't. I have to go alone."

"Tell me why?"

I could hear the roar of off-road vehicles coming from Michael's room, along with shouts of victory. He would be wearing his headphones so he wouldn't overhear. I looked at Carver and nodded. "I'll tell you, but only if you promise to keep this between us."

"I swear it," he agreed. "I won't tell anyone."

I lowered my voice. "The circle had been meant for my son. The men who took Evan said they got hair from my house with the intention of using it to take Michael. They accidentally got some of Evan's as well, but they said they had more spells ready to go, and they would take Michael if I didn't come alone." My eyes were hot, and when I blinked, tears leaked down my cheeks.

Carver reached out and caught one with his finger. I watched as the wet droplet absorbed into his skin, then his eyes turned into clear, watery orbs.

"Carver..."

He blinked as his eyes returned to their dark brown color. "I saw your memory of their conversation with you, Iris. I understand why you're afraid to seek help. I also felt the deep love you have for your son and your need to protect him." He leaned forward, placing his elbows on the table. "But if you're dead, you can't protect anyone. And if you go alone tonight, that's exactly what happens."

I sat down and spread my hands as I fought back more tears. "What else can I do?"

"Trust that your friends have your best interests. Trust that they won't do anything that would put your son at risk. You've created a powerful team, Iris, don't try to play the game alone."

I cocked a brow at him. "A sports metaphor?"

He gave me a lopsided grin. "Put us in, coach. We're ready to play."

"Okay, Credence Clearwater, I get it. Don't go alone, blah, blah. I don't suppose this goddess of yours gave you a few alternative scenarios?"

"No, only that you weren't to go alone."

"Lovely. She sounds about as helpful as my grimoire." My temple throbbed. I massaged it as I considered what Carver said. If the voice in his head was right, then going alone would be the ultimate bad decision. I shook my head. "I have to protect Michael."

"Once you're dead, who will protect him?" The question stung, but Carver's voice was gentle. "It's rhetorical. You are going to rely on the same people you're cutting out of the process now."

I spun my phone in a circle. Bob put a paw on my hand. I scooped him into my arms and cradled him like a baby. "I don't know what to do." I scratched his belly. "What should I do, my cuddly little pumpkin of love?"

Carver, who was not my cuddly pumpkin of love, said, "We can all figure it out together."

I tapped my phone screen and put in my lock code. It was Michael's birthday. After, I called Keir.

He picked up on the first ring. "Hello."

53

"Hi," I said. "It's me."

"I know," he said. "That's why I answered."

"Can you come over?"

"Has she finally come to her senses?" Lu asked in the background. "Is she ready to tell us what the hell is going on?"

Carver smirked.

I made a face. "Tell Lu to come as well. Maybe you should get Zev here, too. I think I'm going to need the whole calvary."

"I'm glad you called." He managed to sound emotionally distant and relieved at the same time. "We'll be there in a few minutes."

He hung up. I looked at Carver. "I hope you're right about this."

"The only other option is death. At least this way, you have a fighting chance."

"A fighting chance for what?" Michael asked. I hadn't noticed that he'd come out of his room. "Don't leave me out of the loop, Mom. I have a right to know." He glanced at Carver. "And who's the new guy?"

"Carver," I said. "Meet my son Michael. He got his father's beauty and my brains."

Carver stood up and offered Michael a hand. "It's nice to meet you."

Michael eyeballed Carver skeptically. "So, what are you?"

"Direct." Carver took his hand back. "I'm your basic eclectic witch with a healthy dash of naiad." When Michael looked confused, Carver added, "A water nymph."

"What's an eclectic witch?"

"I wasn't born with magic, but I learned how to wield it through studying multiple forms of witchcraft and other types of magic."

"Like a sorcerer."

Carver shook his head. "I didn't gain magic by stealing it from others. It's a slippery slope."

"What is?"

"Taking things you haven't earned."

Michael seemed to take in the information for a moment before finally shrugging. "Cool." The shrug was meant to be nonchalant, but I could tell he was more interested in what Carver was saying than he was letting on. "Can anyone learn what you do?"

"Maybe not exactly what I do, but everyone has a connection to the world around them, and with enough sacrifice and discipline, they can tap into that power and build from it." Carver tapped his chin. "What are you really good at? Something that you find easy that others might have difficulty with?"

"Football," Michael said instantly. "Well, sports in general. Videogames, too."

"Natural athletic ability combined with good hand-eye coordination could manifest as the makings of a strong spell weaver. The ancient art of manipulating the threads of magical energy that are in everything around us and the crafting of powerful spells from them. It takes a deft hand to tap into the ability and years of practice to become a novice practitioner and a lifetime to become a master. It's why humans rarely waste their time. And there's always a chance it will never manifest the way they want." He peered closely at Michael. "Being eclectic is not a life chosen easily, and it's not for anyone with bigger dreams outside of the work. There are those who work to live and those who live for the work. If you're not the latter when it comes to magic, then it's better not to start down that road."

"I want to learn," Michael said, shocking the hell out of me.

"Whoa, now," I told him. "As interesting as I found Carver's TED talk, I don't think he meant that you should become an eclectic witch."

Carver gave Michael a curious look. "My curiosity about craft started from a young age, but I began to consider it seriously at your age." He took his wallet out of his back pocket and produced a business card. It was black, and his name, Carver Martin, was embossed in silver. On the back were his phone number and email. "You can call me if you ever want to talk more."

My frown deepened. "You should talk to me first."

"Jesus, Mom," Michael complained. "I'm already up to my eyeballs in all this stuff. Don't you think I have a right to learn all I can so that I'm not as unprepared as you were when your tru-craft sparked?"

I wanted to be angry at his sass, but he was right. I'd been heartily unprepared. I didn't want that for Michael. Besides, he was already in danger, and protecting him was only going to get harder once he graduated and started a life away from me. "Fine," I said. "You may call Carver." I raised a finger. "However..."

Michael groaned. "There's always a but."

"This is a however not a but. I want you to give it a really good think before you call Carver."

He rolled his eyes, then walked over and hugged my neck from behind. "Thanks."

I patted his hands. "Don't thank me yet."

"So, what's this fighting chance you were talking about?"

Now it was my turn to groan. The doorbell chimed. I wiggled my brows. "Saved by the proverbial bell."

I got up and practically raced from the kitchen. I opened the door, and it took a second for my brain to register what I was seeing.

"Well, you going to stand there gawking, or are you going to invite us in?" Dahlia asked.

"We're not vampires," Rose quipped. "We don't need an invitation."

"Hey, sis." Rowan kissed my cheek as he passed me by. He tapped Goldie's fishbowl. "Cute fish."

Next came Marigold, Zev, Lu, and Keir.

"What the heck?" I mouthed.

Keir mouthed, "Sorry."

Lu snorted a laugh and smacked me on the shoulder. "You said to bring the calvary. Welp, the calvary has arrived."

CHAPTER 7

"CARVER?" KEIR SAID WHEN HE SAW THE ECLECTIC witch. "What is he doing here?"

"Divine messenger," I offered as an explanation. "His goddess told him to come." My sisters and my brother were doling out hugs to my son as they piled into the kitchen. The room shrank in size at the sheer volume of occupying Everlees. "I'm going to need a bigger table," I muttered.

"And I'm going to need more information about this divine message," Keir said.

"You're going to be mad at me."

"I already am, so it won't be a new thing."

I couldn't tell if he was kidding or not. "I'm sorry," I said, then more loudly, I announced, "If everyone has a seat, I'll tell you why I called."

"You mean why Luanne called," Rose snipped. She didn't look happy with me either. Had the Everlees and the Quinns got together to discuss me? Or was this just Rose being hormonal because of her pregnancy?

Either way, Lu was going to get an earful from me later. But first, introductions were in order. "Everyone, this is Carver Martin. He's an eclectic witch and a new friend." I pointed to each one of my siblings who Carver hadn't met yet. "Carver, this is Dahlia, Rose, and Rowan."

Carver smiled. "You have a wonderful mix of auras in your family. No two alike, and yet, there is something binding between you and your siblings."

"Maybe because we were adopted," Rowan said. "And what do you mean by auras?"

"We're bundles of energy. That energy gives off...." He wiggled his fingers, palms facing each other. "It's like a haze, though. That's not quite right either."

"Like heat coming off the sidewalk after an August rain," Dahlia supplied.

Carver's eyes brightened. "Yes, very much like that, but add in color, movement, and volume. You all are a rainbow, and yet, your movement and volumes are very similar." He wiggled his mouth and scrunched his nose as he mused on the revelation. "Interesting."

"Sure," Luanne quipped. "Scintillating. Now, get on with what's really going on and why we're just now hearing about it?"

Okay, so Luanne was officially mad at me too. I had to push the care aside. My intentions had been to protect Michael, and if they couldn't understand why, then that was their problem, not mine.

"Evan was magically kidnapped. The guys or gals, or whatever they are, took him by accident. Their real target had been Michael."

There was a collective murmur of utterances from the group.

I held up my hand. "Exactly." I swallowed the hot anger rising in my throat. I rushed through the rest so that I wouldn't have time to stop and scream during the recitation. "Michael was the target. They texted me to call and warned me that Evan would die if I let anyone know. When I called them, they told me they'd gotten hair samples from my house and felt confident that at least one of the samples was Michael's and that if I didn't come alone to meet them tonight at midnight, they would get the next spell right and take my son." I balled my hands into fists and cursed the tears starting to fall. "They were in my house. They took hair samples from my son in order to make me come to them. It was only a fluke that some of Evan's hair ended up in their hands and that they grabbed him by mistake."

"Wait?" Michael's tone was terse. "They were trying to get me, and not Dad?"

"That makes a lot more sense," Marigold said. "I mean, who in their right mind is going to think that Evan was Iris's Achilles' heel."

"That's why you sent me away," Keir said.

I nodded. "I didn't want to, but I...." I gave him a pleading look. "It was for Michael." Keir wrapped his arms around me, and I allowed myself the comfort. "I'm so sorry for not telling you."

"What's Carver's part in all this?" he asked.

"I got a message that Iris needed me and that if she went alone, she would die."

"How long ago did you get this message?" Marigold asked.

"Shortly after you called me, but I was ordered to give the message in person. So, I dropped everything and drove down."

Luanne crossed her arms. "No way you made it from Michigan in five hours."

He gave her a tired look. "I was in Tennessee, west of Nashville, for a job. I broke a few speeding laws but made good time."

I'd had enough of Lu's attitude. "Can you not take your anger at me out on Carver? He is the only reason I called you guys, so he's not the bad guy here. I am."

"You are a mother," Rose said fiercely. "I would do the same for my boys in a heartbeat. You all better just believe." She was crying now, which started my waterworks. Damn it, Rose and her freaking hormones! Even so, I never loved my sister more.

"Thank you, Rose."

Dahlia's blue-green hazel eyes were alight with curiosity. "How did they take Evan?"

Carver fielded the question. "I'm pretty sure they used a translocation spell that targets a person's unique DNA."

"Is that like when all those monsters were coming after the pixies for their dust?" she asked.

Keir gave my sister an assessing look. "I imagine it's very much like that."

Carver raised a quizzical brow at me. I explained. "It was before you. The pixies were having their mating season, and we had a lot of monsters following the dust frequency to find them."

"Exactly." Dahlia bounced excitedly on her toes. "I mean, wouldn't that work?"

"Wouldn't what work?" I asked.

"We can create that energy field again, like the one we did around the pixies to block the signal until they had their babies. We just need to put it around Michael instead. That keeps him safe while you guys," she gestured to Keir, Carver, and me, "do what you need to do."

I blinked rapidly at my brilliant sister, then turned to Keir. "Could that work? Could a magical barrier like what we did during the fruit-bark rites keep Michael safe from a translocation spell?"

When Keir didn't answer quickly enough, I pivoted to Carver. He tilted his head from one side to the other. "I'd have to see the spell, but it sounds like it could work."

Rowan's phone chimed. "Sorry." He nervously pushed his glasses up his nose. "It's my ten o'clock alarm. I was supposed to work the overnight at the E.D. tonight." He looked at Carver and explained, "I'm a doctor."

"Do you need to call them?" I asked.

"No." He finger-combed his short red hair. "I called in the minute Luanne threw up the bat signal."

In that moment, I felt such overwhelming gratitude but also a serious urgency. "The meeting spot is Grave Hall," I told them. "I have to be there at midnight. Which means we have less than an hour to figure out how to modify the spell to protect Michael and execute it before I get on the road."

"Grave Hall?" Marigold sounded alarmed. "At that time of night, and with all the low-hanging clouds. You're going to be lucky if you're able to see five feet in front of the car. That drive is dangerous even when you're not rushing."

"I know," I said. "But I didn't pick the location."

"The only thing up there is some scenic bluffs and a handful of cabins," Dahlia added. "Why do they want you to meet there?"

"Isn't there a legend about Grave Hall?" Rowan mused. "Something about a free love cult who lived up there until they threw themselves off the side of the mountain."

"Oh, yeah," Marigold said. "That was in the sixties, well before our time."

"We don't have time for history lessons," I said. "We need to have the spell together in forty-five minutes." I prayed we had enough supplies. "I have the amber stones we need." I had them charging on a selenite plate in my bedroom. Linda's suggestion. "I'll need powder and mint. Enough for the five of us."

Thomas had said I needed at least five people for the spell to work. I'd had seven when we'd saved the pixies. My siblings, Keir, Luanne, and myself. That evening, they'd become my coven. But I would need both Zev and Luanne for their tactical skills, Keir for his brute force as a puca, and Carver, for his understanding of magic. That left only four behind to keep the spell going. Someone was going to have to stay behind.

"I need five people to keep the spell going while I'm gone," I said. I let the question of who would stay behind linger in the air. "Rowan, Dahlia, Rose, and Marigold can't keep it up on their own."

Michael cleared his throat. "I can do it."

"No," I said dismissively. "I don't want you—"

"Involved?" He sighed. "Mom, that ship has sailed. I'm not a child anymore. And I want to help. If everyone is putting their necks out for me, then I have a right to decide how much I get to be involved. Besides, you have a better shot at kicking those guys' asses with Aunt Lu, Keir, and Zev." He acknowledged Carver. "Him, too."

"When did you get so smart?"

"Good genes," he said. "Besides, if I do this, then maybe I'll finally get to meet Linda." He lowered his lids. "You know when you find her."

"Where is Linda?" Dahlia asked. "I just thought she wasn't in here because of the kid."

"We found a badger," Marigold told us. "He said that he would get the word out to the mountain that you were looking for Linda's donsy. He seemed confident that Morlan would get the message."

"How soon?" I asked. It would take a load off my mind to find Linda safe and sound.

"I don't know. Badgers apparently have a weird sense of time. It could be hours, or it could be days. I'm keeping my fingers crossed that Morlan or Linda will show up soon."

Rose frowned. "What happened to Linda?"

"It's a story for later," I said. "Time is ticking, and we have a spell to modify."

CHAPTER 8

"THIS SPELL IS CLEVER, IRIS." CARVER LOOKED OVER the notes in my grimoire. "It combines earth and air elements and manages to cloak everything inside the circle as if it doesn't exist."

"Just like a Klingon cloaking device," Rowan said.

Carver cocked his head at my brother. "Only because they got it from the Romulans, so technically, it's a Romulan cloaking device."

"I don't care if it's a Jedi cloaking device," Luanne said. "As long as it works."

My siblings and my son all gave her a look of incredulity.

"That's not even the same universe," Marigold chided.

Lu rolled her eyes. "Goddess, save me from nerds."

She wasn't wrong. Us Everlees were nerds and geeks from way back, and we'd grown up with science fiction and fantasy shows. I'd passed the love down to my son.

"Mixing Star Trek up with Star Wars is going too far,

Lu," Rose said. "When this is all over, you're coming over to my house for a movie marathon with the boys."

"I think I'm busy that weekend," Lu joked. She and Rose had become besties over the past few months, and I knew that if Rose planned a day for them, Lu would make sure her schedule was open.

"Anyhoo," I interrupted. "We need to get back on track."

"Sorry," Carver said. "I didn't mean to get us off track. I'm very impressed with your spell craft, Iris. For someone so new to magic, you have a talent for seeing the possibilities. That takes a real gift."

"Iris has always been a problem solver," Rowan said. "Out of all of us, she always seems to plan ten steps ahead of any eventuality."

"She also always seems to know when something will or won't work," Marigold added. "She's always been gifted that way."

Sometimes it wasn't a blessing. In the past, I'd had a tendency to butt into a problem even when the person dealing with the problem didn't want my help. It didn't matter that I could see they were on the wrong path. People don't always want to be rescued. I had to learn how to respect that. Lucky for Michael. He got the Iris who knew how to keep her mouth shut...mostly.

Zev and Keir had made a quick grocery run.

"I got six loose face powders from the health and beauty aisle and fresh mint from the produce area." He handed the bags to Marigold.

"Thank you," I told him. There was still tension between us, but I knew Keir well enough by now to know he wouldn't start a fight, at least not until we found out who was after me this time and why?

"I think we're about ready," I told the room. "We should perform the spell in the house instead of outside. I think it will last longer if it's not at the mercy of the wind." I'd asked Fair Konig right away if his people would help. He'd been eager to be of service. "We need to move all the furniture out of the living room, and I'll draw a pentagram."

"I have ritual chalk in my kit," Carver offered. "It makes a spell more sticky if that makes sense."

"You know more than I do, so I'll take your word for it." Intuition only got you so far. It was nice having someone around who was a real expert in magic, even if he wasn't a tru-craft witch. A lot of principals were the same. "I've modified the wording of the spell to block Michael's signal, for lack of a better word. If I get this right, it should make him, and everyone in the circle, completely undetectable to magic."

Marigold put her hand on my shoulder. "You got it right."

I nodded. "The pixies will keep the powder circulating in this area, and without the wind carrying the powder away, they should be able to keep the barrier going for a few hours." I hoped.

We needed enough time to get up the mountain and beat these bastards at their own game. The plan was for me to drive ahead. Keir, Lu, Zev, and Carver would follow in Luanne's van, hanging back far enough to look like just another traveler at night. I'd given them directions to the cabin off double A road, a mile on the left. Luanne and

Carver would set up a barrage of weapons, both magical and tactical, and Zev and Keir would go deep woods and circle in at the rear. Zev and Keir, being supernatural creatures, could move more quietly and quickly through a dense forest and rugged hillside. I, of course, would go in the front door just like the kidnappers expected.

Fair Konig tapped at my kitchen window. I opened the door, and he flew inside with four dozen other pixies, a mixture of male and female, including his wife Annibish and their daughter Iverlee. The tiny pixie landed on my shoulder. My gosh, she was already almost as big as her parents. "Hello, there."

"Hello, Iris Everlee," she replied. "I welcome the warmth of your home."

"You are always welcome," I told her. It was about twenty minutes to eleven, and we were rapidly losing time. "Are we ready?"

There was a series of excited cheers, squeaks, and clicks from the pixies. My siblings and Michael looked equally eager. They'd experienced a breath of my magic, and the experience had been transformative. I didn't blame them for their excitement. I'd had a choice to lose my magic to potentially save my life instead of participating in the *malificionito* trials. I'd chosen potential death instead. Tru-craft and the elements were mine now, and I wouldn't give them up, not even to save my life. Would I give it up if Michael's life was in the balance? Yes. But it would be more difficult than I wanted to admit.

Rowan, Zev, Lu, and Marigold moved all my living room furniture to the walls. The one small area rug was tossed onto the couch. Carver had gone out to his car and retrieved a leather-bound case covered in glyphs and alchemy symbols—what he called his kit. He opened the cryptic lock, then unlatched the bag.

From a small pouch, he withdrew a piece of chalk and handed it to me. "It's a combination of yarrow, white sandalwood, and ash powder mixed with mica, iron fillings, and lodestone. It is strong for drawing rituals." He gestured to the three-inch long, one-inch squared gray chalk. "You can keep that one."

With my earth magic, I could feel the energy emanating from the gift. I suppressed a giddiness that rose in me. Now wasn't the time to get excited about a new toy. "Thank you, Carver. I appreciate it."

As well as I could, I freehanded a five-point star, then drew a circle around it, connecting all the points. I gave Rowan, Dahlia, Rose, Marigold, and Michael each an amber stone, a sprig of mint, and a compact of face powder. We took the lids off and removed the vented screens.

"Okay, everyone. Michael has to stay in the circle, but you all can make food and comfort runs in and out for yourselves and him," I reminded them before we got started.

"We got it the first dozen times you told us," Rose said.

"Michael, I hope you peed."

"Come on, Mom," he complained.

"Fine, but if it gets uncomfortable later, don't blame me."

I went to the center of the star with my own set of ingredients. "I'm ready to begin." I held my hands up. My family, who had taken up each of the five points on the star, copied my actions. "I'll say the incantation once, and then you guys can join in, okay?"

They agreed.

"*In this circle, there is trust that binds. Energy shared from hearts and minds.*" I centered my thoughts on the people I loved who were in this circle. I knew each and every one of them loved Michael almost as much as I did, and I didn't doubt that any one of them would protect him with their very lives. Dahlia, my rod of strength. Rowan, our reed that bends but does not break. Rose, the glue that kept us together. Marigold, the joy of life. And finally, Michael, my baby, who was almost a man. He was the breath of life for me. With these five in place, I started the spell. "*Northwind blows, no sight to see, no sound to hear. Inside this barrier, no spell can come near. If danger seeks my son, keep him hidden in plain sight so that he can be found by none.*"

I repeated the spell and focused on the pentagram, crystallizing my intention in my mind. I repeated the words. "*In this circle, there is trust that binds. Energy shared from hearts and minds. Northwind blows, no sight to see, no sound to hear. Inside this barrier, no spell can come near. If danger seeks my son, keep him hidden in plain sight, so that he can be found by none.*"

My family repeated my words, and I could feel their intention as their energy filled me. I gathered all that they gave me, and I sent it back out to them in return.

After we spoke the incantation one more time, I commanded them to "Release the powder."

I threw a handful of my own into the air. The rest of my coven did the same. "Bend to my will," I demanded.

The powder shimmered as the pixies flew in circles around and inside the pentagram to keep the powder floating.

Michael's eyes widened, the smile on his face making his dimples the deepest I'd seen them in a long time. He was experiencing what it meant to be coven. I remembered how wonderful it felt the first time I cast a spell with my family, and it felt just as amazing now.

My brother and my sisters all stared at each other and began to laugh with joy as the moment, once again, took us.

We couldn't hear anything outside the circle, but Keir's waving caught my eye. He tapped his wrist. Crap. Bliss would have to wait. It was go-time.

CHAPTER 9

LUANNE HAD WALKIE-TALKIES WITH A THIRTY-MILE radius on flat terrain. Our cell phones would lose service at a certain point the higher we climbed, so the two-way radios would be our only means of communicating at a distance. With the tall trees and winding mountain roads, she warned me that we needed to keep within five miles of each other.

The one she'd given me had an earpiece, and I'd put it in the interior jacket pocket. I doubted seriously if I would be frisked. I don't think the man on the other end of the phone expected me to put up a fight. Boy, was he ever wrong.

All I had to do was tap the earpiece to connect with my team. Once, if it was clear to speak. Two quick taps would mean all-clear but radio silence. Three taps would signal them to send in the rescue brigade, guns and magic blazing. The goal was to act as scared as possible and get as much information out of them while they believed they had me where they wanted me. Acting scared was the easy part. These men, or whoever they were, had snatched a human being using powerful magic right out of my living room and right in front of me. I'd been powerless to do anything. In other words, I was scared. No acting required.

"Iris, can you hear me?" Lu's voice crackled over the radio. "Mic check."

I tapped my earpiece once. "I hear you loud and mostly clear."

"Keep it simple," she came back.

"Fine. I hear you."

"Great."

My heart picked up the pace when the next voice I heard was Keir's. "You can do this," he told me. "You are a god eater."

I smiled. "You say the sweetest things," I responded.

"You're a badass witch, Iris," Lu added. "Don't you forget it!"

I tapped my earpiece. "Heard and appreciated."

At the fifteen-mile mark, my headlights bounced off the fog, and the road became too hazy and incandescent to see properly. I reduced my speed even more. Damn it. I was going to be late, and I feared they would try and make good on their promise to snatch Michael. I trusted my spell to hold up, but it would ruin our plan if they realized they had no power over me.

I didn't know if it would work, but I called air and water for an assist. Clouds and fog were both made from invisible water vapor that condenses into masses of tiny droplets light enough to carry on the air. I kept that in mind as I solidified my intention.

"*Fog and clouds hit the gas, be a pal and let me pass. Ahead and behind, be a dear and keep it clear. I am short on time, so forgive the lousy rhyme. I have a date with fate, and I can't be late.*" Suddenly, the fog grew even heavier, and I cursed my rotten spell for doing the opposite of what I wanted. Then just as suddenly, the fog parted like the Red Sea, and I could see as far as the road allowed, and I was pleasantly surprised that it stayed clear behind me when I looked in my rearview. Score two for team nero and aero-craft.

I sped up, and the fog stayed out of my way the entire distance. At this pace, I would get to the cabin with minutes to spare. Yay? Did I want minutes to spare?

I thought about the look of pure pleasure on Michael's face when he'd experienced the spell. He had accepted our new reality so readily, even quicker than I had, it made me wonder if he really had been born to it. If Carver could teach him how to use and respect magic, Michael would have a much easier time if his tru-craft powers ever sparked.

When, I amended. The fire god Volres said he'd felt the spark in Michael, and he'd basically told me that if I wasn't willing to be his meat suit, he would take Michael when the time came. That had been his first and last mistake. Rose had been right about the ferocity of mothers. I taught that demi-god that you don't mess with my kid, not if you want to live. The thought made me less afraid of what was coming. These bastards had tried to take Michael. They were the ones who should be afraid of me. Not the other way around.

Eight minutes later, Keir asked, "Did you do that with the road?"

"Yep," I answered.

"Lu sends her regards."

I grinned. "Message received." I was pleased that the road behind me had stayed clear. "See you at the top."

"Be careful."

"Back at you. All of you."

My stomach clenched when I saw the sign for Grave Hall. There were narrow strips of land on both sides of the road that stretched for half a mile full of grave markers and headstones. According to Wiki-now, the turn of the century cemetery had its last burial performed in 1926. The small township was established in 1935, and it had been given the name Grave Hall for obvious reasons. I was basically driving down a hall of graves. I'd been through the place once, years ago, but there was rarely any reason to go this far up into the mountain. The people who lived or visited either liked being alone or they liked to hunt. Neither of those things was my jam.

I saw the sign up ahead for double A road. I tapped the earpiece. "I'm closing in. About a mile from the destination."

"Hold up," Lu said. "We'll park on the side of the road at the edge of the cemetery, and I'll let you know when we are ready to go."

Nervously, I tugged at my earlobe. My car clock read 11:55. It would take me a minute or two to get down to the cabin, and that put me right on the cusp of midnight. "Negative," I said. "It's almost midnight. If I'm not on time, this plan goes to shit."

"Wait for us, Iris," Keir insisted. "You have no idea what these guys have cooked up for you. What if they pull a fast one and jump you out of there with a spell like they did with Evan? They could've grabbed your hair samples as well."

I hadn't thought of that. If they wanted me, why go for my son? Why not just grab some of my hair? I shed hair like crazy. I had to clean my hair brush a couple of times a week. Most of the time, I marveled I wasn't bald. It wouldn't have been hard for them to locate a few stray follicles of mine. So why didn't they? The answer: because they couldn't. "Their spell wouldn't work on me," I told Lu. "If they could've, they would've. They wouldn't have needed Michael to lure me up here."

There was no reply. It was hard to argue with sound logic. Still, it was another reason for Keir to be unhappy with me. I wasn't a soothsayer, but I saw a long, unpleasant talk in my future. As they say, it is better to ask forgiveness than permission.

When I pulled up to the cabin, there were two trucks and a van out front. It was now 11:58 pm. I would wait one minute for my backup to get where they needed to be, but regardless of their location, I wouldn't jeopardize our one chance to learn who was after me now. Did these guys work for Bogmall? Or were they just more rando-power-hungry-dicks trying to make a quick magic score at my expense?

Tick-tick-tick. I watched uneasily as the eight turned into a nine. I tapped my mic. "Going in."

Keir responded. "I love you." He didn't sound happy about it.

"I love you back." The absurdity of my life elicited an unwarranted and inappropriate giggle. Not that long ago,

I'd been Iris Callahan, wife and mother. Then Iris Everlee, recently divorced single mom. Of all the future selves I could imagine, none had come close to what I was now. A tru-craft witch with five elements and a world of monsters eager to take them from me. It was time to find out which monsters wanted me this time.

I got out of the car and made a noisy display of slamming the door. I wanted them to know I was here, that I'd made it with a minute to spare. There was no room for mistakes. Not if I wanted my ace in the hole to count.

No one greeted me outside. I went up two rickety wooden steps to a small stoop in front of the cabin door. I focused on keeping calm as I knocked on the front door.

A small man, probably five foot five, maybe shorter, answered the door. He had a long beard that looked like a bib over his gray cloak. His cowl was back on his shoulders, and he had a forehead that took up most of the top of his head. In the middle of all that baldness was a scar in the shape of a circle with three curly swirls like little waves. Was this a Hecate wheel?

I recognized one of the men inside the cabin. He'd been at Iron Grove during my testing. Shit. These were druids. Nope. The only druids allowed were the ones in my coven. All the rest of them could take a flying leap to Hell.

I stepped back, and I must've been heavy-footed because the second stair down snapped, sending me windmilling backward. The small druid grabbed my wrists, and when he did, I felt my magic slam down as if I'd been cut off from the flow of its energy. I tried to get my hands free, so I could press my earpiece a gazillion times for a rescue, but two more men came at me from behind and yanked my arms behind my back. I let out a cry of pain as they twisted my shoulder.

"Bring her in," a man said. I recognized his voice from the phone call.

They dragged me, kicking and screaming, inside the cabin. Then Tiny stuffed a rag into my mouth. After one of the brutes holding me kicked the back of my knee, I slammed to the musty floor. Oh, goddess, help me. The trap for me had been well-baited and well-set.

The room was lit with oil lanterns, and the flickering flames made the situation even more intense. I tried to reach for the flame with my ignis-craft, but it wasn't there. I called to the wood beneath me, but it was as dead as my magic. Had the fog returned? Would Keir find me in time?

With the rag in my mouth, I couldn't even ask the bastards what they wanted with me, though it wasn't hard to guess. They tied my ankles and wrists, then lifted me up and set me in a wooden chair.

A large, cloaked man stepped out of the shadows. I couldn't see his face, but he made a gesture to the small one, who took the rag from my mouth.

"I'm going to kill you," I threatened them. "You are going to regret the day you decided to fuck with me."

There was a chuckle behind me. The large man pulled back his hood, and I felt the blood drain away from my face. Brown hair, neatly trimmed brows, wide mouth, easy smile. My heart boomed in my chest as I recognized my captor. "Derrick?" Derrick Asher was the Green Grove archdruid, and he'd been the only one of those jerks I'd been able to tolerate. Why was he here now? I'd passed their tests. Were they still afraid I was dangerous? "Why are you doing this?"

"The day of celebration is finally here, Iris. The day has arrived for you to fulfill the promise of your birth."

"And what promise is that?"

"To gift me with your power."

Sour bile burned my throat. "Uh, that would be a big fat no from me," I said. "I'm not giving you shit." I rocked side to side, struggling to escape. The chair fell over, but it didn't bust. Not cool. "Let me go, you megalomaniac!"

Derrick squatted next to me, and he raised my chin with two fingers.

I met his gaze.

"Dear, child," he said with a sweet coo. "How does the phrase go? I brought you into this world, and I will be the one to take you out."

Sickness filled my belly, and my mouth watered with fear and disgust. "What do you mean?"

"Haven't you figured it out?" He smiled his friendly smile. "I'm your father, Iris, and I've been searching for you since the day you were born."

CHAPTER 10

THE DRUIDS UNTIED MY HANDS, THEN CUT MY JACKET off. It, along with the walkie-talkie, had been left on the cabin floor. Next, they stuffed the rag back into my mouth again and dragged me out the back door of the cabin and down a path between the trees. Oh, my gawd, I'd been here before. The moon was full and a rusty orange color. A blood moon. No, this couldn't be. The last time I was here, it had been in a dream or maybe a vision. There had been another woman. A tru-craft witch.

When we exited the tree line, instead of an open field, the altar was situated on a rocky cliff. "Welcome to Devil's Lookout," Derrick said to me. "He gestured toward the altar. It was made of four stacked slabs. The shiny white stones glimmer in the moonlight, making the altar seem ethereal and supernatural.

"Ready the gift," Derrick said.

A tall, thin man with a long scraggly red beard and dark, beady eyes waved a bony hand in a "this way" gesture. I gawped when I recognized him as the one who had performed the ceremony in my vision at Iron Grove.

I thrashed about as they tied me down, but there were too many of them and not enough of me, and with my magic shackled somehow, I couldn't find a way to escape. "Please," I tried to plead through the cloth gag. They ignored me. I was a thing, a tool to be used, and not a person to them.

The smoke from the sage burned my nose, and I caught the scent of frankincense and lemongrass. No, no, no. I knew what was coming, and I was powerless to stop it.

They tied my wrists and ankles to four iron rings at the four corners of the altar. I craned my head back, hyperextending my neck, and saw Redbeard standing behind me. I shook my head. "Don't," I tried to say, but my plea was muffled.

He set three bowls on one side of my head and two on the other. He took what looked like a smooth tiger eye stone from the first bowl and positioned it at the point where my thighs met my groin. I bucked, throwing the stone off me.

"Stop it," Derrick said. "Unless you want your son to take your place."

Tears leaked from my eyes as I began to shake. I had to trust that Keir and the others were on their way.

Beardo circled his hands over the stone, his head tilted to the moon, and said, "*Tera des anu modred caltha wen.*"

Next, he scooped liquid from the second bowl and

squeezed his fist over my stomach as if he were anointing me with the water.

"*Nero des anu modred caltha wen.*"

I screamed into the gag again when he placed a live coal from the third bowl on my chest. The cherry red coal cooked my skin, and the smell of burnt flesh made my stomach turn. I glared at Derrick, swearing he would die a horrible death over and over once Keir and the others arrived to save the day.

"*Ignis des anu modred caltha wen.*"

Please, I begged the universe. *Please make them stop.*

The red-bearded asshole inhaled smoke from a pipe and blew it across my face. I blinked as the acrid vapors burned my eyes.

"*Aero des anu modred Caltha wen.*"

That's when the bloodletting began. This ceremony was coming to an end, which meant I was coming to an end.

Not like this, I thought. I can't end like this. I was a lion. Lions don't lie down and die. They roar. I'd proven it over and over again, so why couldn't I break whatever spell or charm they'd used on me now?

Redbeard took blood from each one of his sycophantic minions and used the blood to draw a circle with a dot on my forehead.

I heard a familiar howl of rage and fury in the distance. It was Keir. He was trying to find me. Derrick must've seen the hope in my eyes because he said, "It's too late. They won't find you in time to save you, child." He leaned in close, and I could smell his minty breath. "You're not the only one who can erect a barrier spell.

Reading about the way you solved the pixie hunt problem was truly enlightening. But take solace in knowing that you will live on in all of us." He gestured around at the other druids.

Well, shit. I heard Keir howling and ripping up boards and tearing down walls. He'd probably found my jacket in the cabin and was tearing the place apart to find me. Especially if Derrick had found a way to copy my spell and, by the sound of it, improved upon it.

"*Anima des anu modred Caltha wen*," Redbeard continued.

There was a murmur of agreement before the druids joined their voices in an aria to the heavens. Redbeard touched my cheek, and I turned my head sharply.

The bronze woman was lying next to me. How? Could they see her?

"Blood of my blood," she said. "Down the path, you must fall. If you want to live, you must heed the call."

The words were almost identical to the grimoire's warning.

Blood of my blood, down a path you will fall.

Tears of my tears, you must heed the call.

Between life and death is the divine. To master spirit, you must walk a line.

Summon strength from both Fade and Bright, or you will lose yourself in the coming fight.

Goddess, help you.

Between life and death was the divine. Was the bronze woman divine? Where was this line I needed to walk? And how was I supposed to summon strength from both Fade and Bright when I'd been cut off from my magic?

"The magic is still in you," the bronze woman said. "Hurry."

A little hint as to how to hurry would've been really freaking great about now.

My eyes widened as Redbeard picked up the bone knife he'd used to cut all his buddies' hands and held it above my face. "We thank you for your gifts, *benna-soito*." He leaned over and placed his mouth inches from my forehead. I squirmed, thinking he was going to kiss me. Instead, he glanced around at his moon-singing brothers, their eyes raised to the sky, then whispered, "this is for your sister."

I jerked my head away, but not before I saw the hint of a smile playing on his thin, evil lips.

In my final moments, I reached for peace, for Zen, for a miracle. That miracle landed square on my chest in the form of a thirty-pound, butthole-less cat name Bob.

Redbeard squawked his surprise as Bob hissed and lurched for his face. The rest of the druids scrambled, trying to subdue my chonky-chonky, but to no avail. The imp might be chunky, but he was fast. With razor precision, he managed to throw all the druids into disarray while managing to sever the ropes binding me to the iron rings.

"Run," the bronze lady sang. "Take the leap." She pointed toward the cliff. "It is the only way to stop the ritual."

This was crazy. Nuts, even. Still, I hastily yanked the gag from my mouth, slid off the altar, and got to my feet. There were ten druids between me and the cabin, ready to take me down. Without my magic, I didn't have much of a chance. And considering these guys were ancient and got regular juice-ups from tru-craft witches, my odds were even worse. Bob, my furry hero, was already running toward the cliff.

Down the path, you will fall. Eeep. This was a terrible idea, but I gave over the lesser of two evils, and I sprinted after my familiar. When I got to the edge, I forced myself to push all fear away, and I jumped. The satisfying shouts of dismay from the druids were my only comfort as I plummeted a hundred feet or more to my death.

Then Bob appeared in my arms in my final moments, and the world went black.

CHAPTER 11

I DON'T REMEMBER THE IMPACT OF HITTING THE ground below. A blessing, to be sure. Still, it had felt as if my life and death had been anticlimactic. At least those druid dicks hadn't gotten my magic. It was the only consolation. Well, that and the fact that I hadn't been alone. My delicious Bob stayed with me to the end. A true and loyal companion.

Now I was in a small room that gleamed with blue light. Someone had laid me on top of a stack of pillows and soft blankets. I scanned the area and noticed that the circular room had cloth walls, and the ceiling was vaulted with a round opening. Above the opening was a blue-black ceiling, or was it a sky filled with millions of fairy lights? Was I really dead? Was this the afterlife? Did they have yurts in the afterlife? Because, on second inspection, I was fairly certain this was a yurt.

A movement in my peripheral vision drew my attention. I pivoted my gaze as a dark specter moved inside the room. I reached for my magic, but it wasn't there.

Damn it. What had Asher and his pack of druids done to me?

A giant shadow figure with bright, luminous orange eyes blinked at me. In some ways, it reminded me of the wraith that had driven all the joy from me a month earlier. Only this ghastly creature didn't make me sad or scared. On the contrary, I felt relaxed and calm in its presence. Every part of my intellect screamed at me to run, but I couldn't get my emotions on board.

Because I'm no fool, no matter how I felt, I crawled backward when the creature slithered in my direction. It stopped and then focused its giant orange orbs on me as if waiting for me to do or say something.

"Who are you?" I asked. "What are you?"

The specter's eyes widened, and its pointy ears twitched, and in a voice that resembled Keanu Reeves in *Bill and Ted's Excellent Adventures*, the monster said, "Tis I, fair Iris. Your Bob-a-licious."

I blinked as I tried to process. "My what?"

Its ears flattened. "Your chonky-chonky cuddle monkey."

It was my turn to blink. "I don't understand."

"I am your lovey-lovey, nummy-nummy little muffin of love." Its orange eyes quivered as if on the verge of crying. "Do you not recognize me?"

"My Bob?" I asked with disbelief.

"Yeeeess," he hissed happily. "I am your Bob." He stood to his full height, and his tail swished behind him.

"How did we get here?" I asked him. "How are you talking to me? And why aren't you a cat?"

"I transported you from your world to mine," he

replied. "We're in Amicaregnum, the imp shadow realm, and this is my first form. I am this when I am here, and I am your Bob on the earth realm."

"Amicaregnum? Are we still in Arkansas?"

Bob's laugh was bubbly. "We are everywhere, and we are nowhere. This plane of existence, like most spirit realms, exists in an overlap with your world."

I got to my feet. I was wearing a silk shift dress that draped down past my knees. "Where are my clothes?"

"They were bloody, and your top was burned. Grathilde lent you one of her gowns."

"Grathilde?" I looked around for another figure. There was only Bob.

"My sister," he replied as if saying, *duh*.

I had many questions, starting with, "You have a sister?"

"I have many sisters. Brothers too."

"How many are many?" I asked. I had three sisters and a brother, and I thought that was a lot.

"I haven't counted, but in the hundreds, if I had to guess." The dark creature shrugged. Seeing such a human gesture on a non-human figure was strange. "I only keep in touch with a few dozen."

"How can there be so many of them?"

Bob's tail curled around his waist. "I was born almost a thousand years ago, and imp breeding pairs have at least two litters yearly."

My eyes widened. "Litters?"

"We mate in our chosen animal forms on earth. It is the only way."

What I knew about imps was based on the information Linda had given me when Bob first came into my life. She'd told me that they were empty vessels, tools for witches, and not much good for anything else. But Bob was a sentient being with siblings, some of whom he considered his favorites. She'd gotten it so wrong. Bob was a fully developed being that I'd been treating like my own therapy pet. One thing she'd gotten right, though, was the procreation part. "Do you have a mate?" I asked him.

He snickered. "No. Only imps without witches become part of a breeding pair."

"But you said you'd been around for almost a thousand years."

"Tis true, Iris, but I have always been your familiar. I just had to wait until you needed me."

"For a thousand years?"

"A few years less than that, but yes."

I looked around the room and noticed a table with a decanter of what I imagined was some liquor or wine with a couple of goblets on a small table. There was a large mirror with a swatch of turquoise fabric hanging loosely over one side. "Is this where you go when you aren't with me?"

He nodded. "It's my home."

"And how do you always seem to know when I need you the most?"

Bob gestured to the mirror. "I wait, and I watch, and when you need me, I come."

"With the mirror?"

"Yes." He glided over and took the blue cloth off the frame. "It's a conduit to your world."

The floor was heated and felt good against my cold toes as I joined Bob. "You can watch from here."

He nodded. "Watch and travel."

"Like a portal?"

"Like a portal," he agreed. I could hear the pride in his voice. "I have one of the biggest portals in all the realm."

I tried not to laugh. "I guess sometimes size does matter."

He didn't hold back. His laugh was joyous. Surprised at how solid he felt, I put my hand on his arm. He looked like a shadow with glowing eyes, but his body was corporeal.

"Babsildo," a high-pitched voice called from outside the yurt. "Hurry. They're here!"

Panic popped my calm like a spike against a water balloon. "Who's here?"

Bob's gleaming eyes narrowed. "Not a who." His eyes widened, reminding me so much of Cat-Bob. "It's a what. Come see." He took my hand and dragged me outside.

The imp realm was full of mountains that carved out space in the sparkling night sky. I'd never seen so many stars, and while there wasn't a moon, there was enough light to see.

"How is your sky so bright?" I asked him.

"There's no artificial light on this plane, so natural light is abundant." He pointed to the sky. "It's about to start."

"What is—" Before I could finish my question, the stars began to streak across the sky. "Oh, my gosh."

"It happens daily, but it never gets boring," he said. "It is called the stellostendia."

"How does it happen?"

"It's the crossing of souls when the dead gather for their final journey."

I blinked as thousands of lights streaked across the sky. "Really?"

He nodded. "I believe so."

"Bob, you said you brought us here? But how? Could you always do that?"

His dark ears twitched back and forth. "Your magic acted on my ability to transport myself, making it great enough to pull you into this realm with me. Without your power, it would've been impossible."

"But Asher had cut off my magic." And considering I'd never crossed into another realm before, I wasn't sure how I'd managed to pull this one out of my ass. "Help me understand."

"You are finally becoming," Bob said. "I felt the anima spark in you. It called to me. For a little while, I couldn't feel you or see you at all. I'd worried you had passed on to your next life. I would have missed you."

"You felt the anima?" Had the bronze lady triggered my fifth element again? "How? The druids cut me off from my magic."

Bob held both hands, palms up. "I don't know about your other magic, but imps are creatures of spirit magic," Bob said as if it were as plain as the nose on my face. "I've been waiting for this moment since you sparked to tera-craft."

"Waiting for what?"

"For you to become everything you were born to be."

"This sounds like some sands through the hourglass

bullshit, Bob." I was beginning to hate all this destiny stuff, but with my familiar around, it was hard to be anything but calm. Still....

I could hear the smile in his voice. "It's time to go home."

"How? I told you that my magic isn't working." I tried to call on stone, flame, wind, and water. None of them answered. "It's gone." The realization was devastating.

"Not gone," Bob said. He put his arms around me, and my calm returned. "Just entangled. But your anima-craft is alive in you. I can feel it."

"I'm not sure that helps. I can't feel it. If I can't feel it, I can't wield it. And even if I could, I have no idea how to use it."

Bob patted my back. "I will guide you."

Every element, I'd been put in the path of someone who could teach me. I looked up at Bob as understanding dawned on me. "Are you my spirit guardian?"

"Yes," he said. "I thought you knew."

"I did not, but I'm glad," I told him. "I'm glad it's you."

He gave me one last pat, then let me go. "Come." He retook my hand and led me back into his home.

We stood in front of the mirror, and I stared at our reflections. My hair stood on end, my cheek was swollen, and I looked like I'd been put through the wringer. After moments of feeling sorry for myself, I asked, "Well? Am I supposed to be doing something here?"

"Look into the mirror," Bob instructed.

"I have been," I complained.

"Relax your eyes," he said. "Look past what you see and think about home."

My dentist had one of the magic eye posters that looked like a bunch of squiggly patterns, but if you looked at it just right, you could see dolphins jumping out of the water. There had been instructions to move close and cross your eyes, then move back from the picture as you let your gaze drift as if looking at something distant on the image's horizon. I tried the technique while also thinking about my house. It was hard to stay focused on both.

"It's not working," I told Bob.

"You can do this, Iris. I believe in you," he said encouragingly.

If Linda had been instructing me, she would've pelted me a half dozen times and told me to get on with it. I didn't always love her method, but she got results. God, I missed her. My pulse ratcheted up a notch when the mirror's surface began to spin. I grabbed Bob's arm. "Something is happening," I told him.

"Hold your focus," he guided. "Try to sort the important from the unimportant."

"Important stuff only," I said. "Got it." That sounded easier said than done.

Images were whirling and flitting by so fast it was hard to grab any of them.

"Don't force it, Iris," Bob said. "Let go of your need to control the situation. Spirit cannot be forced. You have to let it simply exist."

His method for tapping into the fifth element seemed

like a lot of hokum. Still, I forced myself to stop manipulating the situation and let the images reveal themselves.

"Think about what you want. What is it you want to see the most? Anima is soul craft. If you are honest with yourself, it will do your bidding."

I fought back my frustration. If Bogmall could make anima work, then why couldn't I? What was it that I really wanted? I shook my arms out, forcing myself to relax. "This would be easier if you were a big ball of orange and white fluff."

"I'll always be your ball of orange and white fluff," he said soothingly. "But first, we must get you home."

"Home," I repeated. I thought of my son, Keir, my house, and my garden. Those were the things that made the location home for me. When a pink image entered the eddy, I latched onto it without thinking. "Linda," I said. "Bob, I see Linda."

She grew more defined as some of the other images faded. There were chunks of her missing. Parts of her hat, her nose, the tops of her winklepickers. I stared with horror at the state the snotgurgle had left her in. "Linda," I called. "Where are you? Tell me how to find you."

Her mouth moved, her expression angry, but I couldn't hear what she was saying. I imagined it was a string of curses ending with "*Stupid, Kleinkind!*"

"Does this mean she's still alive?" I turned a frantic look at Bob. I'd been worried that she was dead but had been afraid to voice the fear.

"She is still living," Bob said. "But she is stuck." His eyelids lowered to slits.

"How do I unstuck her?"

"Getting yourself home would be a good start."

I gave him a peevish look, then turned back to the mirror. Linda was gone. I let my eyes drift again as I focused on family, love, and home, reminding myself that home would get me one step closer to finding my missing gnome.

I saw Keir's face, eyes black, and expression full of rage and grief as he carried a body...was that my body? Then I saw Marigold. She was crying. Was I dead?

"I'm not," I said aloud. "I'm alive."

"Of course you are," Bob said. "Keep going, Iris. Get yourself home."

I had to get back to my family. They were mourning for me, but I was still here. Like Linda, I survived. I was just..., what had Bob said, stuck. Was this the line between life and death that the grimoire had spoken of? It had said to call upon both Fade and Bright to master spirit.

When learning the first four elements, I found I could use a part of myself as a sacrifice to make the magic work. Tera-craft responded to bone and minerals, and ignis was satisfied with my blood. Aero used the oxygen in my body, while nero had a lot of water to choose from. What would spirit require? The soul, of course. I concentrated on the part of me that was responsible for logic and emotion. These things made an individual more than a collection of physical parts. I called to that piece of me, and I felt it answer.

I stared into my eyes as the mirror's surface churned and rippled. *"Take me back to where it began,"* I intoned.

"Safe at home, as was the plan. Let the journey be fast, so I can escape this past and be with my loved ones again."

The mirror turned black. I shot Bob a panicked glance.

Then I was standing in my living room at the center of my drawn chalk circle. My siblings and my son were smiling and laughing. I let out a massive sigh of relief as I sagged to the floor with exhaustion. "I made it."

"You sure did," Marigold said. "It's wonderful." Pixies were flying around, kicking up dust. How long had I been gone? It had felt like an eternity, but if my family was still holding the spell, it couldn't have been much longer than a few hours.

The pure joy on Michael's face made my heart dance. I was home. Safe and sound. I searched for Keir. He was outside the circle, waving his arms and tapping his wrist.

I walked past Rowan and stepped out of the circle. My palms began to sweat. "What time is it?" I asked.

"It's ten to eleven," Keir said. "We better get moving."

"Moving where?" I asked as the situation became more apparent.

"Grave Hall," he replied. He narrowed his gaze on me. "Are you all right?"

Holy crap. I didn't know how it was possible, but I'd not only traveled home, I'd rewound the clock. I was getting a second chance. I smiled at Keir. "I'm more than all right, and those bastards are not going to see me coming."

CHAPTER 12

"What's going on, Iris?" Keir asked. "We should get going. The roads will be thick with fog and hard to get through. Time is short as it is."

I grinned. "The roads won't be a problem."

"And why is that?" Luanne asked.

"Because we've already traveled them, and I know I can clear the way." I waved off their concern. "You guys are right. We don't have much time, but we need another plan. When I get to the cabin, a bunch of druids are waiting on me. The first one I see grabs my wrists, and whatever he did, or will do, cuts me completely off from my magic."

Keir leaned forward. "I don't—"

I held up my hand. "I love you, but you have to listen to me so I can get this all out. The original plan isn't going to work. We've already gone once, and it ended with me on a sacrificial altar and you guys unable to find me. Derrick Asher modified my barrier spell and crafted one for himself. He has it set up around the altar area, and he doesn't need a bunch of pixies to keep it going."

"Asher?" Luanne asked. "You think Archdruid Asher is a part of this?"

"I don't think." I was getting frustrated. "He is a part of it. Hell, he's probably the guy in charge. Though, Redbeard seemed pretty important."

Luanne scoffed. "This sounds like a fantasy."

"Or a vision, maybe," Zev suggested. "Maybe she has seen the future."

"I didn't see it. I lived it," I reiterated. And Redbeard had said something about my sister. Was Bogmall in league with these druids? Did she know Derrick Asher was our biological father? Asher had talked about my mother in the past tense, as well. Had he sacrificed her for magic? He mentioned that he'd only put it off because she was pregnant. Until now, I'd been satisfied to never know more about my birth mother. My adoptive parents had given me a wonderful life.

I hadn't had any questions for the woman who had left me at a hospital on the other side of the mountain. But Asher's plans for me put another spin on why she might have relinquished custody. Had she found out her lover's plans for her child? I know I would do anything for Michael. Giving him up to hide and protect him would be the ultimate sacrifice. Was Bogmall really my sister? If she was, why hadn't my mother kept us together? Had she kept the blonde bitch with her or placed her somewhere else? Either way, it made the whole situation even more personal.

"An important tidbit," I added. "It turns out that Asher is my biological father."

"How do you know that?" Keir asked.

"Because he told me."

"This is starting to sound like that Star Trek show you love." She made her voice sound Darth Vadar-y. "Iris...I am your father."

I fixed her with a flat stare. "How many times are you going to mix up Star Wars and Star Trek?"

She gave me a bland look. "Until it stops driving you nuts."

I didn't have time for her shenanigans. "Carver, do you have anything in that kit of yours to stop whatever they used to block my magic?"

"Maybe. If I knew what they used to block your magic in the first place."

Bob jumped up on my lap. "Oh, my sweet boy. You were there. You helped me so much."

Keir and Luanne looked confounded.

"After I jumped off the cliff, Bob took me to the imp realm. Amicaregnum." I hoped I pronounced it correctly. "He's my spirit guardian." I smiled as he rolled onto his back and began to purr earnestly as I scratched his belly. "Thank you, my chonky-butter-muffin."

Zev gave the little imp a skeptical look. "Bob is your guardian."

"Imps are spirit creatures. They live in the plane right below where souls pass on to their next life." The way they'd traveled across the imp sky like shooting stars had been nothing short of amazing. "It was like watching a miracle."

"You saw it?" Keir asked.

I pivoted to face him as Bob got up onto the table. I took Keir's hands. "I have experienced many wondrous things since my tru-craft sparked, and seeing souls fly to their next destination was top ten." I smiled at him. "But you're my number one." I squeezed his fingers. "Tell me you believe me. I can't watch you grieve for me again."

"I believe you," he said. He pressed his warm palm to my face. "We'll make a new plan."

"Better get on the stick then," Lu said. "We are almost out of time."

I quickly walked Carver through the small druid, grabbing my wrists and the feeling of being instantly cut off from my magic. "I don't know if he had something in his hands that he put on me or if the spell was somehow connected to the cabin. My power was instantly gone the moment he touched me."

"Hmmm." Carver's eyes pivoted up as if in deep thought. When his gaze met mine again, he asked, "Can I have some of your saliva?"

"Dude." Lu made a face. "That's gross."

I frowned at her. "My spit is not gross."

"What do you want it for?" Keir asked him.

"I can see Iris's memories through the water in her body. It's either tears, spit, blood, or urine. Since she's not crying, saliva seems like the least...." He glanced at Luanne. "Gross. Maybe if I can access the memory of this future event, I will notice something important that her mind dismissed as insignificant."

"I'm game to try. It might be the most expedient way for someone to believe me, too."

Keir said, "I told you I believe you. I've experienced the future through visions my whole life."

"This wasn't a vision," I told him. "I'm telling you, it happened." I took Carver's hand and turned it over so that his palm was facing up. "You sure about this?" I asked him.

He nodded. "Go ahead."

I gathered saliva in my mouth and deposited the sample into his hand. The liquid was instantly absorbed. Carver's eyes turned into orbs of water as his body entered a trance-like state.

When his eyes normalized, he stared at Bob.

"Yep," I said. "Pretty wild, huh?"

"Wild is an oversimplification, but you were right about the amazing part." Carver got up and washed his hands. "I'll never think about imps in the same way."

"What about the magic blocking spell?" Keir asked grumpily.

"It was a simple transfer spell. Iris was blocked the moment the bald man touched her. He had a scar on his head." Carver drew the circle with the three swirl-wave-looking design in the middle that I'd noticed right before all hell had broken loose. "That's the Wheel of Taranis."

"Taranis?" Keir swore under his breath. "Taranis worship has been banned for years in our ranks. If there is a practicing cult in our territory, Freya needs to know about it."

I shook my head. "Not tonight, she doesn't."

Lu scowled. "If this is a Taranis cult, we need to go the full-nuclear option on those human-sacrificing cannibals."

"This also means they probably aren't praying to

Hecate for their energy to power their spell." Carver sounded relieved his goddess wasn't responsible for the kidnapping translocation spell. "And it makes more sense why she would guide me to you."

"Well, she wasn't wrong about me going it alone. I can't go back to that cabin with you three miles away. I have the advantage of knowing their plan for me. Two men grabbed me from behind. I didn't see them, so they must have hidden near the front." I looked at Zev, his fire magic was gone, but he could still pop himself from one location to the next. "They have a barrier spell around their altar. It's just down the hill out the back of the cabin. Asher called it Devil's Lookout."

"I still think we should just firebomb the entire area," Lu said. "That would take care of Daddy-dearest and all his Oompa-Loompas."

I had questions, and Asher was the only one who could answer them. But was knowing the truth about my origins worth risking my life and the life of the people I loved? "Do you think that blowing them up will negate the spell they made to take Michael?" I shifted my gaze to the barrier bubble, thankful that my son couldn't hear our conversation. I didn't want him to know what the arch-druid had planned for him or me. "Asher threatened to sacrifice Michael in my place if I didn't cooperate. If he finds a way to escape, I'm afraid he'll punish me through my son. If we do this, we have to be sure that Derrick Asher is vaporized off the face of the earth."

Keir put his hand on my shoulder. "Let's plan on the go. It's fifteen after, and we're going to be cutting it close, even without the fog."

"I'll drive my van," Lu said. "I have too many weapons and ammo to transfer over to your car, but I'll park at the end of the double A, only a mile away instead of five miles. I can cover that space in a tick, plus it will give us an escape vehicle if we have to un-ass if the situation goes tits up." She arched a brow at Carver and me. "For the non-tactical folk, that means, in case we have to get the hell out of dodge if the mission goes ten kinds of wrong."

"I figured," Carver said.

"I'm good with context clues," I concurred. "Okay, so Carver and Keir are with me. Zev and Lu take the van. Zev can transport you both to the cabin."

"I can." Zev's gaze narrowed. "But I cannot guarantee Lu's safety without seeing where we will land."

"Just stick to the road, fire boy," Lu ribbed him. "Can't go wrong with open pavement."

"Okay. We have a plan." It felt as if we were breaking a huddle. "Lu and Zev, the coms worked all the way up the mountain. We won't do anything without checking with you first."

Lu gave me a tight-lipped smile. "And we won't do anything without you either, Mom."

I flipped her off. I waved at my family as we passed through the living room, and I prayed to any goddess listening that I would see them again soon.

All right, I thought. *Grave Hall, take two.*

CHAPTER 13

I COULDN'T SHAKE THE INCREDIBLY FOREBODING SENSE of déjà vu as I sped up the winding road toward Grave Hall. I'd spent the first five minutes of the drive convincing the Quinn siblings to let me go into the cabin first. I believed that more information could be gained by allowing Derrick to take me. They'd finally agreed, but only if Carver could figure out a charm to break their magic buster spell. I'd accepted the terms. It might seem reckless, but I wanted to know what happened to my mother. I believed she was dead and needed to know Asher's role in her death. Also, he was the only one who might know about Bogmall. According to her, she'd been born before me.

Poor, poor, Iris. Always one step behind me. Just like the day we were born. She'd telepathically told me this while I was submerged in salt water and on the verge of drowning. Stupid cow. Even if we shared the same womb, as far as I was concerned, she could go straight to Hell. Do not pass go. Do not collect two hundred dollars. Blood did not make us kin. The same with Asher. He'd already shown his colors. He had no interest in being a father then or now. All he wanted was my magic. They both wanted it, and I planned to give it to them on full blast.

Keir was in the passenger seat, looking up reference books using Darling U's online library. We'd lose signal soon, so his thumbs were getting a workout. Carver sat in the backseat, opening and closing little bags, vials, and other sundries from his kit.

I heard a triumphant "yes" from him, and I hoped that meant he'd found a charm to block the blocking spell at the cabin.

"What's good?" I asked. "Did you find a nullifying spell?"

"No," he replied. "However, I have hyssop, worm-wood, and vetiver, along with clover oil and eye of newt."

"Ewww. Is that a salamander eye or something equally disgusting?"

"Nope." Carver chuckled. "It's something used to make my favorite condiment."

"It's mustard seed," Keir said absently as he scrolled his phone.

"Spoilsport," Carver told him. "Anyways, I can't make a blocking spell with these."

"Then why the excitement?" I couldn't hide my disap-pointment.

Carver clucked his tongue. "Because I think I can do you one better. It will require some of your magic to acti-vate, but I believe between the two of us, I can create a mojo bag that will bounce any spell directed at you onto the caster."

"Seriously?" I tightened my grip on the steering wheel. "That would be awesome."

"Are you sure it will work?" Keir asked, suddenly interested.

"We can test it after it's completed. It shouldn't take me more than five minutes to bless and assemble the ingredients. Iris will need to bind the ingredients with either earth or water. Both might even be better."

"Why those two?" I asked. "You're a water element, so I get that, but why earth as well?"

"Fire and wind are volatile. This spell requires energy that is grounded in the feminine. Earth and water have movement, but they're slow-moving elements that lend themselves to receiving. We need that calming energy to complete the charm. If we were building a bomb, that would be a whole 'nother story."

I was learning a lot about magic from Carver. If I survived this, maybe Michael and I would both start lessons with the eclectic witch.

"Can I get a bomb bag too?"

He laughed, but when I didn't join in, he asked, "Are you serious?"

"Yes," I said. "I'd like a 'break in case of emergency' ready-to-go weapon. If for some reason the bounce-bag doesn't work, I'm going to be left without any magic."

"It's a good idea," Keir said with the first hint of enthusiasm. I'd give him a break. Since I'd told him about dying the first time I'd faced the archdruid of Green Grove, he'd been struggling to keep his tarry-eyed puca in check.

"Fine," Carver agreed. "I can make you a magic bomb,

but make sure you are clear of the radius when it goes off because it won't discriminate its targets."

I gave him a thumbs up over my shoulder. "We're about ten minutes from Grave Hall, so do it quick."

"Damn it," Keir cursed. His nail had grown into a black diamond claw, cutting a jagged scratch across his screen.

"I'm okay," I said. "I'm not going anywhere."

"His eyes flickered between pitch black to their normal white with gray irises. "You already did."

"And I came back."

"And you are tempting fate all over again."

He was upset. Understandable. His feelings were valid. I'd be angry, too, if he kept putting himself in harm's way. Unfortunately, harm was actively seeking me out. I couldn't stay home and avoid it. I loved Keir, and I hated that I was putting him through the wringer. He loved me, so I hoped he understood that there wasn't any other way.

He set his broken phone down and looked at me with his soulful eyes, his soft kissable lips in a grim line. He had the kind of face, handsome without being overly rugged, pretty without being overly feminine. I would never, no matter how long I lived, get tired of looking at his face.

"What are you thinking?" he asked.

"I'm thinking that when this is over, I'd like to spend the rest of my life with you."

Keir's brow dipped, and the crease between his eyes deepened. "Are you asking me to marry you?"

My whole body should have been screaming, Danger, Will Robinson! Abort. After all, I had only been divorced for a few months, and my ex-husband was already engaged. People might think I was having a knee-jerk reaction to the news by jumping into a new relationship too quickly. But my love for Keir surpassed any I'd ever felt for Evan, and he loved me better than anyone in the world. As much as he wanted to protect me, he also let me face my own challenges and fight my own battles. And he had my back, even when he was mad at me.

I smiled.

Like now.

On top of all that, the man had a body that I could happily lick up and down on the daily. He was that delicious: tall, slender, narrow hips, tight ass, and thighs that could crack walnuts, though I hadn't tested the theory. Being a shifter helped him maintain his beautiful physique. But even better than his outer beauty was his inside beauty.

"Would that be something you want?" I asked, finally addressing his question.

His eyes went full puca, and his ears began to elongate. "Let's talk about it after we kick druid ass."

"I've finished the bounce charm," Carver interrupted.

I reached over my shoulder, and he put it in my hand. "Mmm," I said. "Smells spicy." My stomach rumbled, and I realized I hadn't eaten all day. "I wish it didn't smell like food, though."

Keir dug into a small backpack he'd brought along and pulled out an energy bar. Salted caramel, chocolate, and pecan granola. My favorite. "You really are the best."

"I know," he said, and I could tell some of his earlier anger had waned. At least the anger he'd been harboring toward me.

"Don't open that bar until you complete the charm," Carver warned. "You don't want food ingredients changing the spell unpredictably."

"Got it." I wedged the bar between my mid-thighs and held the bag up. "Just add water or earth?"

"Yep," Carver confirmed. "Use Bright magic. Creation will work better to keep the energy balance needed for the spell to work."

"You used Fade and Bright?" I asked. "I had thought it was particular to tru-craft."

"Most magic has a light and dark side, or a creation and a destruction path. But you're right that only tru-craft witches are sparked to one or the other, and in rare instances like yourself, both. Thomas taught me about your magic. It's not something I can tap into, but I value knowledge almost as much."

Good old Thomas. Carver's dad and my favorite snitch. I still liked him, but he wasn't off the hook for ratting me out to Freya. I held the bag on the steering wheel, so I could keep driving while I activated the mojo. "I'm glad Lu's in the other vehicle," I said as I used my thumb to wipe spit from my tongue and swiped it onto the bag. I focused my energy on moving the liquid into the coarsely woven sackcloth and made it disperse inside with all the ingredients.

"Done," I told him. "How do I know if it works?"

Carver hit me in the back of the head with a coin and shouted, "*rosea capillus transformacio!*"

"Ouch. What the hell, Carver? Some warning next time." I glanced in the rearview mirror. His brown hair had turned shocking pink. I blinked and pursed my lips, trying hard not to laugh. "Uhm...."

"It worked," he acknowledged. Then with a shrug, he added, "I make it work."

I giggled. "You sure do." Out of the corner of my eye, I saw a smile tug at Keir's lips. "Fun spell," I told Carver.

"It was the only one in my kit that I didn't mind getting hit with, and it's temporary."

"How long does it last?"

"A few days," he said. "It's a party trick."

I grinned. "Me thinks someone enjoyed *The Craft* when he was younger."

"Who didn't?" Carver countered. "I'll get to work on the bomb. How much time do we have left?"

Up ahead, I saw the sign for Grave Hall. "We're almost there, with about two minutes to spare, or I'd slow down. Make it fast."

"Working on it," he said. "Goddess, I hope this doesn't blow your fingers off."

"I hope it has more power than that," I said. "I want a bomb, not a firecracker."

"Yeah, yeah," Carver said.

The rows of headstones ramped up my anxiety. It meant we were close. I'd done it before, but it had been terrifying. I pressed a finger against my chest where Redbeard had set the hot coal.

"We could go with plan B and blow them to shit," Keir said, sounding more and more like his sister. "Lu has a rocket launcher. We could even do it at a safe distance."

As tempting as it sounded, I declined. "I have to know about my mother and my sister."

"Asher might not know anything."

"Then you can come in, diamond nails a snapping, and cut him to ribbons."

Keir smirked. "I'm on board with that plan."

"I thought you would." I gestured to the backseat as I came up on double A. "Time for you to crawl in the back and hide with Carver. I softened my voice and was only half teasing when I said, "And be nice." He'd had a bug up his butt about Carver since the man had shown up with the message about me not going by myself. You'd think he'd be more grateful. If it hadn't been for Carver, I would've gone alone, and no one would've ever known what had happened to me.

"I'm nice." His expression was bland. He kissed my cheek and said, "Be careful."

"I will," I promised.

Carver tapped my shoulder and handed me a smaller bag. "If you must use it, throw it while running in the opposite direction. It's stable until you say the trigger phrase."

"Got it." I tucked it into my jeans pocket, remembering how they'd cut my jacket off. "What's the phrase?"

He said it very slowly, taking a breath between each word. "*Ignis. In. Foraminis.*"

"Huh," Keir said as he settled down in the back. "Fire in the hole."

"Seriously?" I shook my head. "I'll try and remember."

"If you can't remember," Carver said. "Don't try to use it. The wrong trigger phrase might activate the ingredients in...uhm, unexpected ways."

"Like what?" The cabin was just up ahead. "Never mind," I told him. "Get down."

I tucked the bounce-bag inside my bra, at the bottom near my underwire. They hadn't frisked me last time, so I hoped nothing had changed this time around. I tapped my mic. "You ready?" I asked.

"Parking the van," Lu said. "Be there in two shakes of a djinn."

"See you on the other side."

"Roger that. Don't do anything I would do," she added.

It was her way of telling me to stay safe. "Love you, too, Lu."

I reached my hand to the back and felt Keir take it. He laced his fingers in mine. "Trust that I'll be there."

"I do," I told him. "I love you."

"I love you more," he replied, letting go of my hand. "Go get 'em."

I remembered the energy bar last second and grabbed it as I exited the car. I ripped it open and gobbled it down fast, not even caring that I was still licking chocolate and caramel off my fingers as I made my way to the rickety-ass steps.

Note to self: avoid the second step.

Then I knocked at the cabin door.

CHAPTER 14

THE SAME SHORT MAN ANSWERED THE DOOR. HE HAD A long beard resembling a bib over his gray cloak. His cowl was in the exact same position, off his head, and on his shoulders. I noted the Wheel of Taranis on his forehead. Lu called them cannibals, and I had the sudden urge to yell, "*You're eating people! Soylent green is people!*"

I managed to resist, but just. The last time I'd taken a step back once, I'd realized they were witch-sacrificing druid assholes, but this time, I pushed the little guy aside and walked right in.

It was fun watching the bluster leave Derrick Asher's expression. "Iris," he said, adjusting his stance. "I bet you're surprised to see me."

"Not really," I said, feigning boredom. "What was my mother's name?" I asked. If I only got one question, that was the one I wanted him to answer the most.

Again, he looked like I'd popped his swagger balloon. There was nothing quite so festive as a deflated ego. "What makes you think—"

"I know you're the sperm donor, jackhole. Just tell me my mother's name." Thankfully, I could still feel my magic flowing in my veins. The mojo bag was holding. "If you do, I'll give you what you want."

"And what do you think I want?" he asked.

"My magic, of course. It's what every megalomaniac wants."

He arched a brow. "And you'll give it willingly if I answer your question."

"Well, actually, there are a few questions that I want answered."

"If this were a modern cop show, I'd think you were wearing a wire." He laughed at his jibe. The joke was on him; I was wearing a wire. Sort of. My radio was on, and my backup could hear everything being said. Derrick rolled his hand at me in a grand gesture. "Fine. Ask your questions."

Five or six druids had gathered behind me, most of their faces covered with hoods. I saw a Redbeard's long straggly facial hair sticking out. I didn't have to see his face to know it was him. After watching him kill that poor woman, I hoped he died slowly and horribly.

"Who is my mother?"

"Her name was Heather Goodall."

Was? I guess that confirmed my suspicion. My birth mother was dead. "Did you sacrifice her?"

He raised a brow. "She was mine to do with as I wished," was his reply. I took that as a yes.

"Did she know of your plans for me?"

"Oh, how she ran when she discovered the truth. As badly as she wanted you, I should've known she'd hidden you away. She possessed spirit magic and could see how special you were from the moment you were conceived." He savored the words. "Her power was magnificent, but I know it's a mere dip in your well."

I shuddered at his lively retelling. "And Bogmall?" I asked. "Do you know about her?"

He grinned, his capped teeth gleaming, even in the dimly lit room. I wanted to knock them all out. "Of course, I know about her. For the longest time, I thought she was you." He wagged his finger in my direction. "I didn't know Heather was pregnant with twins. She did a good job of hiding you. Your sister, not so much. Only when she turned eighteen did I realize she didn't have the spark and never would. That's when I knew I got it wrong. I'd been tricked."

"Does she know you're her father?"

"I'm not her father." He spat. "She is a tool. A sharp and useful one. But nothing more. You are the prize, Iris. You always have been."

Okay. I'd heard enough, and I was ready to bolt. "It's been fun, and it's been real, but I can't say it's been real fun." I gave him a two-finger salute. "Adios, asshole."

"Grab her," Derrick ordered his men. "Tie her up." He smiled. "And don't worry, your friends will get here too late. The door has been spelled. No one will be coming to your rescue."

I narrowed my gaze. "You're an idiot." Ignis burned through my blood, and I drew on the power of fire. "They're already here, and I'm ready for you this time." Flames poured down my arms and erupted from my fingertips. The men who'd been coming for me staggered back. No one wanted to feel the burn. "Let's get this pyre started."

The startled expression on Asher's face fueled my ignis-craft. I threw a blazing stream at the archdruid, wielding it like a bullwhip. I snapped it at the last second, blasting a hole into his ceremonial robe.

Surprisingly agile, the archdruid dropped to the floor and scrabbled to hide behind a chair. He shouted, "Stop her!"

I counted eight men in the room with me. I could hear pounding on the door, Keir roaring outside the cabin, and wood cracking as he tried to get inside through the wall. "I will burn this place to the ground with all of you in it," I seethed.

"Your child will pay for this, Iris! The spell," Asher commanded. "Evoke the apportation."

"No!" I threw a blazing ball of righteous anger at him, and it struck the chair with enough force to knock it aside.

I caught sight of Redbeard racing to the back of the cabin. Was he following Asher's orders or running away? Either way, I had to stop him.

Energy rippled at my back. Then there was a sound akin to a sonic boom. I whipped around to see four robed assholes on the floor, blood running from their eyes. Someone had thrown a hefty spell my way, and the mojo had done its job.

"How?" Asher asked.

"Bounce-bag, bitch." The ceiling cracked, and drywall dust scattered around us. My puca was trying to come through the roof. A series of explosions battered at the door, and a gun discharged. Lu and Carver? Where was Zev? Was the magical barrier strong enough to keep a djinn out?

Redbeard drew a circle in the air. I hurled a fireball in his direction, but another druid batted it aside as if it was nothing.

"*Translationem evocation!*" he invoked.

Time seemed to stop for a moment. Nothing happened.

Redbeard's voice was sharp as he repeated, "*Translationem evocation!*"

Again, nothing happened. I remembered Michael was home, safe in a barrier with his aunts and uncle. My son was protected. I couldn't say the same for these jerks. If my friends couldn't get inside, I wondered if the druids could get out.

Another ripple of energy bounced off me, and the druid who had thrown the spell began to writhe and wretch, foaming at the mouth as he clutched his throat.

An old-school taunt popped into my head. "I'm rubber. You're glue. Whatever spell you throw my way bounces off of me and sticks onto you."

The choking man made a gurgling sound and collapsed to the floor.

"Stop attacking her with magic," one of the druids yelled. "Use conventional weapons."

Would the bounce-bag work with bullets? Doubtful. Oh, damn. I slashed flames at the druids between me and the front door, crying out as a bullet struck the back of my thigh.

"Don't kill her," Derrick said. "I need her alive."

He couldn't siphon magic from a dead witch.

I used the fire in my blood to cauterize the wound as I hopped to the door.

A tall, hooded druid, the same one who had batted my fireball away, seemed to come out of nowhere. He kicked me in the side, and I cried out when my ribs cracked under the force of the blow.

The shorty with the scar trained an absurdly large handgun at my head. "If you move even a hair, I will shoot you."

"You can't kill me," I gasped. "Asher..."

"I won't kill you," the little druid said. "But I will shoot your arms, legs, and stomach. You'll survive long enough for the gifting."

It was as if Danny DeVito had been given the role of Dirty Harry. I half expected him to say, "Go ahead, Punk, make my day."

The tide had turned, emboldening Asher to come out of hiding. The tall druid who had kicked the shit out of me moved to stand behind him. "Your death would've been easy," he fumed. "Painless. Not anymore. And when I'm done with you—"

I saw the flash of a bone knife from beneath a robed sleeve as the tall druid thrust the blade in one sharp, smooth movement. It entered the right side of Asher's neck. He looked stunned as he turned to face the druid. More surprise registered in his eyes before he crumpled to the ground.

The druid who'd knifed him in the throat spat on him. And when Asher's killer pushed his hood back, I experienced my own jolt of surprise. It wasn't a man under the heavy cowled robe. It was the blonde hexen-bitch, aka my long-lost twin. "Bogmall," I growled.

She snarled, never taking her eyes off me, as she kicked the dying archdruid in the back. "Who's the tool now? Fucking dick."

The sentiment might be our only common ground. Apparently, we both hated Asher. A handful of the druids left standing made a run for the back door, but several, including Redbeard, went to stand beside their new master.

"You're mine now, Iris. Finally, the wait is over." She waved a finger in the air. "But first."

She knelt beside Asher and lifted him until his bloody head was cradled in her lap. I watched in horror as she leaned over as if to kiss him. Instead, she said some words I couldn't understand. A pale green mist began to flow from the archdruid's parted lips and into Bogmall through her nose and mouth. When the mist dissipated, she shoved him to the ground and flipped her hair back.

"Whew!" she said, wiping her nose as if she'd just done a line of coke. "Good to the last drop."

The intense energy pouring off her stirred up my magic, leaving me tingly and breathless. Until this point, I'd thought Bogmall was a dangerous nuisance. Now, I knew the truth. She wasn't a minor player. She was a big bad, and I would have to take her down soon, or she would kill me.

But not today.

The front door splintered as a blast of magic shattered it to pieces. Lu stepped inside and, without the slightest hesitation, shot Druid DeVito right between his Wheel of Taranis. *Bullseye*.

Keir, in full battle puca mode, tore a gaping hole from the ceiling. He roared his fury as he dropped down into the middle of the cabin. He had razor-sharp teeth, long ears that stood up from either side of his head, and his eyes were pitch black. Pointy antlers, five branches each, were mounted to the top of his skull, and his arms had grown to the size of tree trunks. There were shouts of alarm as he snapped his teeth in the druids' direction.

Zev grabbed a nearby foe and snapped his neck as Lu and Keir fended off spells as they slaughtered the remaining druids.

The pain in my side and my leg had intensified as the onus of the fight shifted to my friends. Bogmall drew a circle in the air, readying some kind of spell. I shouted a warning, but it was too late, she was fading from the room, and she was taking Redbeard with her.

"No!" I couldn't let her get away. My son would never be safe if I let her survive. I couldn't think fast enough to deliver a spell that would break whatever magic she worked, but I did have a bomb. "Get down," I shouted to my team as I dug the small bag from my jeans and threw it at the disappearing sorceress. "*Ignis ferengi!*"

"Oh, shit," I heard Carver say as a noxious gas filled the room. "Everybody out!"

CHAPTER 15

NOT EVEN ZEV'S DJINN POWER COULD REMOVE THE stench of the spell gone rotten egg bad. We'd all had to scrub down with copious amounts of apple cider vinegar and baking soda paste to eliminate the odor. Afterward, we bagged up all the clothing we'd worn and tossed them into the outside trash bins. Showering had helped, but even now, I could still smell whiffs of the putrid sulfuric aroma.

"And then your mom was like, *ignis ferengi*!" Lu, who was in the chair that matched the couch, hooted as she relayed the bomb fiasco from the night before to Michael. She slapped her knee. "Ferengi, of all things!"

Michael, who shared the couch with us, laughed so hard that tears leaked from his eyes. I hadn't heard him let go like that in a long time. It made the jokes at my expense worth it.

Embarrassed, I chuckled and then regretted it. I'd used tera-craft to mend my broken ribs and repair the bullet wound in my leg, but I was still sore. Linda would've done a better job of fixing me while simultaneously giving me ten kinds of hell for getting myself damaged in the first place. Damn, I missed the hateful hussy.

"Don't make me laugh," I complained. "It hurts."

"Not as much as that bomb stank." Lu waved her hand in front of her nose. "I've been sprayed by a skunk before, and this was way more toxic."

After we returned home, Dahlia, Rose, Marigold, and Zev left as soon as the living room had been put back in working order. Lu, Carver, and Rowan had stayed the night. As a doctor, he'd wanted to ensure my injuries healed.

Rowan and Carver were sitting in chairs they'd brought in from the kitchen, and all of us lounging around, even after the awfulness of the night before, was comforting.

"*Ignis in foraminis*," Carver said. "For-ray-minis. The spell called for a fire in the hole, not a fiery alien with a gift for acquisition," he added, referencing Star Trek.

"It sounds like you were lucky all it did was stink." Rowan leaned forward, his elbows on his knees. He looked at Carver. "I'd love to learn more about how you put your charms together. For academic reasons, of course."

"Yeah, sure," Carver said. "I can walk you through it... for academic reasons."

I got the sense that Michael and I wouldn't be the only Everlees getting tutored by Carver.

Lucky for Lu, Rowan, and Keir, my kid was a jock and had plenty of comfy clothes for them to sleep in. Carver was the only one who hadn't needed a pair of sweats and a t-shirt. He had been out of town when he'd been prompted to find me. So, he'd already packed a bag of clothes. He'd worn pajamas to sleep on an old air mattress I purchased years ago. My house was small, but we made it work. Lu slept on the couch, and Rowan and Michael bunked in together.

By the time I got up around ten, Carver had changed into black jeans and a black sweater that contrasted heavily with his newly acquired pink hair. The rest of them were still in Michael's gear.

Rowan got up from his chair. "I'll make breakfast. What do you have in the fridge?"

I hadn't been shopping since before we'd left for Iron Grove. "Chances are good the answer is *not a damn thing.*" I looked at my kid.

"I fried up the rest of the eggs two days ago," Michael said. "Sorry."

Carver said, "I can go get groceries."

Rowan rewarded him with a pleased smile. "I'll go with you." He looked at those of us who were still lumps on the couch. "What are you in the mood for?"

"Waffles," Michael said.

I grinned. "And some bacon."

"Don't forget eggs and cheese," Keir added.

"Maple syrup, the real stuff," Lu jumped in. "Not that fake shit."

Carver raised a brow and grinned. "Your wishes are my command." He bowed with a flourish. With the pink hair, he reminded me of a court jester. "We'll be back shortly."

"I'll pick up some stuff, food and such, for Goldie as

well," Rowan said. I noted that my brother had a little extra giddy-up in his walk.

After the door closed behind them, I glanced over at Lu. "Am I imagining things?"

She smirked. "Nope. I see it too."

Keir frowned. "See what?"

Michael got up.

"Where are you going?"

"To grab a shower and get in a game with Doug."

"You have any plans today?" I was hoping he'd stay close. Bogmall was out there somewhere plotting my demise. But I didn't know where, when, or how she would strike, and it wasn't fair making Michael a captive in the meantime.

"Dad called this morning. I am going to lunch with him later." His expression was guarded. "That's okay, right?"

I nodded. "Of course, it is. Have you talked to him since yesterday?"

"He called this morning to check on me." Michael tugged at his lower lip and then scratched at his patchy morning beard. "He's taking all the magic and witchcraft stuff better than I thought he would."

"Maybe Adam is mellowing him out," I teased.

Michael rolled his eyes. "Whatever." He rubbed his stomach. "Call me when breakfast is ready."

Lu got up next. "I'm going home."

"No breakfast?" I asked.

"I'll be back. I want to get into my own duds. Maybe run a comb through my hair a couple of times."

"I get it." I blew her a kiss because I was too stiff to stand for a hug. "See you in a bit."

When we were alone, I rotated until I was facing Keir, and I curled across his lap.

He wrapped his arms around me and pressed his forehead to mine. "How are you feeling?"

"Like I got run over a couple of times by a bus."

"That good, huh?"

I pressed my cheek against his chest, loving the way his heart hammered whenever we touched. I ran a hand under his shirt to play with the sparse hair. Keir's whole body vibrated with energy as I traced a heart onto his skin. My skin ignited with pleasure as his mouth slanted over mine, and he kissed me in a way that made my head spin. Keir tasted the way I imagined wild magic would, a combination of raw power and energy. And that energy made me wet with desire. I interlaced my fingers behind his neck, deepening the kiss as my desperation for him grew.

I tilted my head back as he kissed down my neck. He traced the midline down my stomach before sliding his fingers past my waistband. He slid his fingertips over my clit, and I squirmed on his lap as the throbbing intensified. I needed Keir like birds need to fly, and when I was with him, I never wanted to land. More than needed, I wanted him. I wanted all of him. His bulge was hard against my hip. I reached down between us and slid my hand over the loose material of the sweatpants and rubbed the length of his generous shaft.

"Now?" he asked. I could feel his grin as our lips melded together. "Here?"

I'd almost forgotten that Michael was in his room and that my brother and Carver would be back. I felt like a teenager weighing the risk of doing it with the possibility of getting caught or not doing it at all. My lady bits definitely voted for doing it.

"Bedroom." I made it a demand as I got up from his lap. He chased me down the hall into my room, grabbed me from behind, and ushered me toward the bed. I giggled with laughter until I heard Michael yelling for Doug to *flank right!*

"Lock the door," I whispered to Keir, then went into the bathroom and grabbed the talc. Quickly, I clapped the powder into the air as I walked a big circle around the bed. *"Beyond these walls, no sound to hear. Within these walls, my words are clear."*

Keir's lip curled, making him look predatory as he stalked over to me. "I'm going to make you howl." He captured my mouth with his, holding me against his lean torso with care. The kiss was devouring and conquering as our tongues intertwined in a dance for dominance. A fight we would both win. His hands roamed my back, my thighs, and my buttocks as if he were memorizing every curve and dip. He broke from the kiss and nuzzled my neck, and I relished the feel of his hot breath sizzling against my skin.

He stripped my shirt off, then my bra. I arched back as I went up on my toes when he cupped my breast and lowered his mouth to claim it. His lips clamped around the puckered nipple, sucking and nibbling, sending shock waves of pleasure through my body.

"You're so beautiful," he murmured as he slid his hand

down my pants again. "So wet." His teeth grazed my nipple as he slipped a finger inside me, and I shuddered as passion burned me like a raging inferno.

"I want..." I panted. "Want...."

His mouth, once again, was hot on my lips, silencing my need. He lifted me up and then gently lowered me onto the bed. My heart pounded like a roar in my ears as he stripped his clothes off, his cock springing hard from his body, and his eyes just bordering on black.

The way he looked at me sent me to the edge of ecstasy. If he didn't hurry, I was going to end up finishing without him. "Oh, shit," I moaned, rushing to get my pants kicked off. I touched myself, and damn, if that didn't turn his eyes pitch black. Mother of gods, the way he wanted me turned me inside out. "Get your sexy ass over here before I orgasm without you." My words sounded strangled to my ears, but I was on fire with pulsating need.

He crawled up my body, and I spread my legs as he nestled his hips between my thighs. I looped my calves around his back, and he thrust inside me. His lips brushed mine, and he tasted so good, and his scent—I breathed him in as I thrust again—masculine, earthy, and so virile. A man. My man.

Every thrust of his rigid length took me to the edge, laying me physically and emotionally bare before him. Keir was mine. *Mine.* Feral grunts and groans coming from both of us echoed off my bedroom walls. The building pressure turned my body into a powder keg, ready to blow. My mouth watered as his power merged with mine, and it was as if our souls had intertwined.

Between the power and the ecstasy, I didn't know where he ended, and I began. It had never felt like this before. Complete. We were complete. I gripped Keir's shoulders, holding on as the first shock of orgasm bowed my back, and I howled as the convulsing pleasure and joy exploded inside me.

Keir's howls joined mine, and I swear I saw the beginnings of antlers poking from his forehead. He shuddered above me as he gave one final thrust.

After, he stared down at me, the black fading from his eyes. His eyes were wide with wonder as he stroked my hair away from my face. "That was...."

"Amazing," I finished.

"I felt you inside me," he said. "I felt myself inside you."

"Well, I hope so," I laughed.

He chuckled. "Not like that. It was like we were together outside our bodies."

"Our souls intertwined."

"Exactly."

I nodded. "I felt it too, but I thought it was just a byproduct of mind-blowing sex." I covered my mouth as a horrible thought popped into my head. "Oh. Oh, no. What if it's my spirit magic? Could I have literally grabbed your soul and forced it to dance with mine?"

Keir snorted a laugh. "I can attest that my soul was willing." He eased from me and rolled to his side. He traced a finger down my chest to my belly button. "We'll figure it out." He kissed me. "We always do."

"I love you," I told him. "And in case I haven't told you lately, it's embarrassing how much I love you."

"You have all of me, Iris. Heart, body, and now, apparently, soul."

I smacked his arm. "Don't tease me."

"I told you I'd make you howl."

I giggled. "At least I didn't grow antlers."

His hands immediately went to his forehead, and I laughed again.

"We're back!" I heard Rowan yell then he said, "Where is everyone?"

Thank you, silence spell.

CHAPTER 16

Michael looked out the living room window. "Dad's here."

I'd kept the bounce-bag from the night before, and I gave it to him. "Take this," I told him. "Keep it in your pocket."

He frowned. "What is it?"

"It's a protection charm. If anyone tries to use magic on you, it will bounce the spell back at them. Carver made it for me."

"Huh." Michael tucked the charm into his front pocket. "Cool." He kissed my cheek. "Thanks, Mom."

"For what?"

"For not treating me like a baby."

"You'll always be my baby," I cooed.

"And now you've ruined it." He rolled his eyes and grinned. "I better go." He opened the door and walked down the sidewalk to meet his father.

I went to the window and watched as they chatted for a moment. Then Michael shrugged and returned to the house with Evan behind him. Great. Ex-husband drama. And the day had started so well.

"Iris," Evan greeted. "I wanted to check in with you. Anymore, uhm, supernatural trouble?"

"Nope. All's good."

Michael gave me a look that said, liar, liar, pants on fire. Whatever. He could tell his dad or not tell his dad whatever he wanted to at this point. I had made peace with Evan knowing about me being a witch. His getting magic-napped had made hiding it from him next to impossible. Thanks, bio-dad, for another shit sandwich.

"Good, good." Evan ran his hands through his curls. "I'm glad you got it under control. Don't want to have to worry about Michael."

"Dad," Michael said. "I told you I was fine."

This must've been part of the sidewalk conversation. "Did you want anything in particular?" I asked my ex.

"No," he said. "I'm just still trying to process everything you told me yesterday. After those men took me, you can't blame me for being scared. I know that losing Michael would be the worst thing you, we, would ever experience."

"Jesus," Michael groaned. "I'm right here. Quit talking about me like I'm not."

Evan's concern made me anxious. Was I being too relaxed about the threat to our family? Maybe my job was to lock Michael somewhere safe and throw away the key. My neck started to itch. Was I getting hives now? Cripes. I needed the two of them to go have lunch before Evan pushed me to the edge with his paranoia.

My sweet Bob began to rub his body against my legs,

purring as if my life depended on it. Thank you, sweet chonky-chonky. I picked up my Bob and cuddled him. He nipped my finger with a love bite.

As chill as possible, I said, "You guys go enjoy lunch. I'm sure nothing will fall apart in the time it takes to eat burgers and fries."

"And a milkshake," Evan added.

"That too," I agreed. "I'll be here when you get back. If you have more questions, you can ask. I can't promise to have all the answers, though."

Evan nodded. "That's fair." He put his hand on Michael's shoulder. "And don't worry, I'll take care of him."

My smile was as tired as I felt. "I know you will."

I'll admit, it was a relief to watch them drive away in Evan's mini-SUV.

Carver, Rowan, Lu, and Keir were in the kitchen. Rowan sipped some tea and said, "And that's why you don't put wires up your urethra." Both Keir and Carver were visibly appalled. Lu, on the other hand, looked amused.

"It was a dude, wasn't it?"

"Without a doubt." Luanne chuckled. "Women are less likely to stick things into their pee holes." She gestured to Rowan. "Your brother entertained us with some horror stories from the emergency room. Like the one about the roach in the—"

I cut her off. "I'm good. No need to hear about the roach or anywhere it might've been." I still had Bob in my arms. I sat down and put him on my lap. "What are we going to do about Bogmall?"

"Until she shows herself, she's a ghost," Lu said. "I've called my connections, and they've called their connections. She's not on a single radar, and she has zero web presence and no credit cards, at least not under her name. I can't even find a parking ticket." She spread her hands wide. "But I didn't come back with nothing. I found out some information about your mother."

I scratched Bob's ears faster. He shook his head but put it right back under my hand after. "You did?"

"Having the name helped. From there, it was easy to track down her social security number. It went inactive forty-two years ago."

"A year after I was born." I was suddenly nervous. "What else?"

"I found an adoption form."

"For me?" I'd always been told I'd been abandoned at a hospital in Briarberry Falls. If there was a form, then my parents had lied to me.

Lu shook her head. "Not for you," she said. "For Heather Goodall. She'd been adopted at birth. The adoption was closed. At nineteen, she petitioned the courts to unseal her adoption records, but the birth mother refused to disclose her identity."

"Ouch," Rowan said. "It's one thing to not want to find your birth mother. It's another to find out your birth mother never wants you to find her."

I looked at my brother. He was five-ten, had dark red hair, blue eyes, a smattering of freckles across his nose, and he'd worn glasses since kindergarten when the teacher discovered that he couldn't read the chalkboard. And, he'd always had a curiosity for science that seemed to elude the rest of us. I wonder how much was from his mother and how much was from his father. "Do you think about finding your birth parents?" I asked him.

He pushed his glasses up his nose and sniffed. "Sometimes. Mainly for health history. I had a patient who was adopted. A seemingly healthy woman in her late forties. She had high blood pressure, and within a year of her diagnosis, she had a stroke and a heart attack. Maybe if she had known her family history, we could've prevented the long road to recovery she's had to endure."

"But not because you want to know people who are related to you by blood?"

He shrugged. "I'm happy with the family I have."

I put my hand out, and he took it. "Me too. Besides, finding your bio family is not all it's cracked up to be. The two I've met both want to kill me. One of them is dead now, but you get the picture. I'm thrilled with the family I got as well."

"I've got more information," Lu said. "Heather Goodall's last known location was Briarberry Falls. She had lived with another woman named Persephone Alexander."

"Briarberry Falls is where I was abandoned as an infant."

Lu nodded. "As luck would have it. Ms. Alexander still lives there."

"You're kidding me."

"Nope." Lu slid a piece of paper with a number on it. "I called her an hour ago to verify that she had known Heather. She says she'll talk to you if you are interested."

I felt numb. A woman living less than two hours away

had known my mother and lived with her, probably while she was pregnant with Bogmall and me. If she could offer any insight into my psycho sister, it was worth the gas, right? So why did I feel like I was breaking a little on the inside?

Two and a half hours later, Keir and I drove to a cottage house in Briarberry Falls. The town, like Southill Village, was steeped in mountain heritage. Persephone Alexander's cottage was a historic house, and a plaque above her mounted mailbox said, *Kindred House, Est. 1899*.

I took a deep breath and then pushed the doorbell. I could hear the chimes playing "Ain't No Mountain High Enough" inside the house.

The door opened, and a black woman with short gray hair, round glasses, and a steady gaze answered. "Hello," she said. "You look just like your mother."

I smiled nervously. "Can we, uhm, come in?"

"Yes." She cast a suspicious eye at Keir. "Do come in, but be warned, I have safeguards around the house."

Okay, not weird at all.

Keir didn't take offense. "I don't mean you any harm," he told her. "I'm here for Iris. Moral support. I can wait in the car if you'd prefer."

She made a show of mulling over his offer and then shook her head. "Do come in. I have tea and cookies."

Ms. Alexander's house was immaculately kept, and her furniture was all early 20th century. She had framed pictures of women lining the hallway walls, including black and white photos that looked like they predated the home. I raised my brows at Keir as if to ask *wtf?* He raised his back at me as if to answer, *hell, if I know*.

The woman wore pearl-beige silk pants with a matching jacket that went to her knees with a salmon pink camisole. She gestured for us to sit at her small kitchen table. There was a wooden box on the surface. "Those are your mother's things. She left them behind when she ran."

"Ran where?" I asked.

"As far away from you as possible," the older woman answered. She took a kettle off the stove and poured hot tea into tiny cups.

Logically, I knew that Heather had been trying to protect me by leaving me behind, but hearing Ms. Alexander say those words stung. "And what about my sister?"

She stopped mid-pour. "What sister?"

"My twin," I said. "My mother gave birth to two daughters. She gave me up, but what do you know about what happened to my sister?"

"Your mother didn't have twins. There was only one child born. That was you."

"That's not true," I said. "I have a twin sister. She was born before me."

Ms. Persephone looked befuddled. "Child, I delivered you into this world right upstairs in the second bedroom on the left, and I promise you that you were the only child in that womb."

Now I was confused. Derrick Asher and Bogmall were under the impression that Bogmall was my sister. My twin. But if Ms. Alexander had been the person to deliver Heather's baby, me, how could both be true?

"I've met her," I told the woman. "She's a horrible

person, but I believe her. For years, our biological father believed she was me."

Her face grayed. "Derrick Asher?"

I nodded. "He's dead."

"Good." Relief eased the wrinkles at the corners of her eyes. "I hope it was painful."

"Not painful enough," I said. I opened the box. Inside were pictures of a woman who did look a lot like me. She had light brown hair, hazel eyes, and a similar build to mine. The images of her when she was pregnant made me smile. One reminded me so much of my pregnancy. There were two rocks in the box. White and black. Fade and bright. There was also a necklace with a circle within a circle. "Spirit."

The woman smiled as she brought the tea over. "Do you know what that means?"

"It's the symbol for the spirit element," I said.

The older woman nodded. "So you know your truth. I wondered if you ever would."

I frowned. "You know about tru-craft."

"Child." She shook her head and pulled her necklace out of her blouse. It was an upside-down triangle with a line through the bottom.

"You are a tera-craft witch."

She tucked her charm away. "What are you?"

"I am tera, ignis, aero, nero, and anima."

She didn't seem shocked. "Your potential was fulfilled, despite your mother's best efforts. Ah well, with Asher dead, you should be safe enough."

"Why did you think I wouldn't?"

"Your mother had powerful spirit magic. She bound

your soul to keep your power from manifesting. She believed it was the only way to keep you safe, but magic has a way," she replied wanly. "Careful of the tea. It's hot."

"And Bogmall?"

The woman narrowed her gaze at me. "Bogmall...." She sighed and blew on her tea. "I can't believe she did it."

"Did what?" Keir asked.

"Heather asked me to make her a clay baby two months before Iris was born. Have you heard of clay babies?"

"No," I told her. "But I'm guessing it's a baby made of clay."

"Your mother wanted me to create an infant out of clay who would look like a cross between her and Asher. She planned to animate the baby long enough for Asher to believe it was you, and then the infant would die within a few weeks. If Asher believed the child to be you, you would be safe. I used my tera-craft to sculpt the child, but I didn't believe it would work." The woman cackled. "She called the clay baby Bohdmall after a druidess from the Irish Fenian Cycle. Your mother was a romantic at heart." She waved the thought away. "Anywho, it takes a god or goddess to create life from clay. I didn't think she would get any of them to answer her prayers. She must've made them an offer they couldn't refuse." She looked suddenly weary. "But I guess she did. Are you saying this babe of clay is still alive?"

"Yes," I said. "Definitely alive, and she's extremely powerful."

The woman leaned across the table and put her hand

over mine. "She's not your sister, Iris. She's an empty vessel that should've never been filled."

"This house," I said. "It's a refuge for tru-craft witches?"

"And other women in need." Ms. Alexander smiled. "I was one of those women once. I stayed, so when Ms. Glenn died in nineteen seventy-eight, she gave me the house to carry on her legacy." Her gaze caught mine. "I'd be pleased if you came back to visit. I don't get much company these days."

"I will," I promised. As long as Bogmall didn't kill me, I planned to keep it. "Now, please tell me everything you remember about my mother. The good, the bad, and the beautiful."

Ms. Alexander grinned. "That I can do, child. That I can do."

CHAPTER 17

I'D LEARNED SO MUCH FROM MS. ALEXANDER, including that my mom had been a fan of Alien with Sigourney Weaver and loved listening to Fleetwood Mac and The Eagles. She'd been a young woman, not much older than my son when Derrick Asher turned her life into a living nightmare, but I was grateful she had Kindred House for a little while. A refuge in the storm.

I was still trying to absorb all the information she'd given me. One of the biggies: Bogmall wasn't my sister. She was a piece of clay molded into something that had become a real living person. How in the world had my mother managed to pull it off? And what god or goddess had assisted her in the miracle? The visit to Briarberry Falls had yielded as many questions as it had answers.

"My mother had been anima-craft," I said as Keir drove us back to Southill Village. I was just learning what it meant to have spirit magic.

"They are some of the most powerful tru-craft witches. A rare breed," he added. "I can see where you get it from." He reached over and put his hand on my thigh. "She sounds like the kind of mother who would do anything to protect her child. Sound familiar?" He squeezed my leg. "It runs in the family."

"You're not still upset with me for not telling you about the phone call, are you?" We hadn't discussed it since last night, and I didn't want us to be the kind of couple that avoided talking about the hard things. That hadn't boded well for me in the past.

"I wasn't upset with you," he said.

"You're not very good at hiding your emotions," I told him. "You were mad at me all night."

He gave me a coy glance. "I wouldn't say *all* night.." I thought he might be referencing the part of the evening that I accidentally proposed, but since he hadn't brought it up again, I'd let it go.

"So, you *were* mad at least part of the night.."

"I was...irritated."

"I'm sorry," I apologized. "I should know better than to hide things like that from you, but I was scared for Michael. As you said, I would do anything to protect him."

"Not telling me wasn't what irritated me. I knew you were keeping information from me when I left. Lu wanted to put a tracker on your car, but I told her we had to trust you."

I arched my brow at him. "Did Lu put a tracker on my car?"

"Probably, but that's beside the point. The point is, I do trust you to make your own decisions. I won't try to control you, not if I can help it."

"Then what got your bits in a bunch?"

"Carver."

"Carver?" I hadn't expected him to bring up the eclectic witch. "Why?"

"Because he convinced you to come clean about what was going on. It's dumb. I'm not jealous, but I'll admit it made me feel a little possessive." He gave me a crooked grin. "I got over it."

"Good," I said. "Honestly, if Carver hadn't told me that a divine goddess had warned me not to go alone, I wouldn't have confessed anything to him or anyone. He wasn't the reason I told you. He was merely the messenger."

"You really saw Bob in his imp form?"

"Oh my gosh, yes, and he was glorious. Imagine Bill from *Bill and Ted's Excellent Adventures* as a humanoid shadow cat. Even better, he's my spirit guardian. He has this giant scrying mirror that he uses to watch me, and it can transport him into his cat form when he comes to our world."

"You love that imp, don't you?"

"I really do. He's better than wine with a Xanax."

Keir shook his head. "This scrying mirror. Can he see everything?"

I flushed as I caught his meaning. "I hope not. I think he only tunes in when I'm upset or anxious. He has a life in his world." My thoughts darkened as I recalled my broken gnome, lost somewhere between realms. "I saw Linda."

His eyes widened. "She's alive?"

"I think so." I rubbed my temples. "She's badly damaged. Maybe beyond repair. I have to try, though."

"How did you see her?"

"Bob's mirror."

"You should get a scrying mirror of your own."

"Can I do that?"

He laughed. "Spirit magic is all about scrying, reading cards, bones, runes, seeing the future, and the past, communing with the dead, and more. You should learn to scry. It sounds like you have a talent for it."

"I think it was mostly Bob," I said. But I did like the idea of getting my own mirror. Maybe we could use our mirrors like walkie-talkies, and he could communicate with me from the imp realm.

"I can see your wheels spinning."

"I'm thinking about how much I enjoyed talking to Bob and having him talk back." I pivoted in the seat to face Keir. "Do you think I could find Linda again with my own mirror?"

"That seems like something you should find out."

For the first time in a week, I started feeling excited. Was Bogmall still a boil on my butt? Yes. Would I allow her to spoil every aspect of my life? No. Besides, the more I learned about my powers, the better able I would be to combat her when the time came.

"Thank you," I told him.

"For what?"

"For loving me so well."

"That's the easiest job I've ever had."

We were driving down the mountain on the Southill Side, and my phone started sending me notifications. I had weather alerts, a missed spam call, and a text from Evan's fiancé Adam.

Is Evan with you? the text read.

It was a strange question. *No*, I typed back. *He took Michael to lunch.* I looked at the time. They'd left for lunch almost five hours earlier. It was close to supper time now.

Haven't heard from him since yesterday morning. Was worried. Thanks for letting me know.

Sorry. Have you tried to call him?

Not answering his phone.

Maybe Evan was processing his feelings about magic and whether he should tell Adam. It would be a hard decision. I know because I'd had to make it with my family and Michael.

I'll call Michael. He should be home.

Thank you. Sorry to bother you.

No worries.

I pulled up my favorites list and tapped Michael's number. After a few rings, the call went to voicemail. I called Evan next. Same thing. Straight to voicemail. My pulse quickened.

"What's wrong?" Keir asked.

"It's Evan and Michael," I said. "Neither of them is answering their phone."

"Maybe they're out of range. There are dead spots all over the mountain."

"Not at my house," I said. "And the motel gets reception as well. There's no good reason for them not to answer." I started panicking again, and Bob found his way to my lap. "Rowan might still be at the house with Carver." I dialed my brother.

He picked up on the first ring. "Hey, sis. Did you find what you were looking for?"

I ignored the question. "Is Michael home?"

"He hasn't gotten back yet. I figured he and Evan were doing some daddy-son stuff. Why?"

"I can't get a hold of him. He's not answering his phone."

"I can drive to the motel and maybe hit some of the business streets and see if they are there. There's probably a reasonable explanation that I'm sure we'll laugh about when they show up."

"Murder's not funny," I told my brother. "And that's exactly what I will do to Evan if he doesn't return my kid."

"Do you think he took off with him?"

"Maybe." I squeezed my eyes shut, forcing my worst fears away. "He talked yesterday like he wanted to take Michael back to St. Louis." But then, wouldn't he have called and told Adam? "Adam hasn't heard from him since yesterday morning. He's worried. I'm worried. It just didn't make any sense."

"I'll drive around and call you if I find them."

"Thanks."

"That's what we do," Rowan said, then hung up.

I let out a frustrated growl. "I don't need this on top of everything else." I clicked my tongue as I remembered something. "Evan lost his phone when he was kidnapped. He didn't have it."

"Okay," Keir nodded. "That explains why he hasn't called Adam."

"Yeah," I agreed. "But it doesn't explain how he called

Michael this morning." A sick feeling washed over me. Evan had been roughed up before his return, but his face was perfect and handsome as ever when he'd arrived at my house. "Or how his cuts and bruises were suddenly healed." On top of that, Bob had been around, and Evan hadn't sneezed one single time. "This can't be happening."

"Tell me," Keir said.

"I think Bogmall is Evan. The same Evan I handed my son over to this afternoon."

CHAPTER 18

By the time we made it to Southill Village twenty minutes later, I'd never been so glad that we had taken a gas-guzzling, climate-killing speed demon of a car instead of Keir's eco-friendly, slow-as-hell, electric Mini Coop. We would have still been slogging down the mountain. I unlocked the door and tried to get out before Keir parked the vehicle. Several cars were at my house—three at the curb and Carver's car in the drive. The ones at the curb were my sisters.

I charged my way inside. "Has anyone found Evan's car?"

"Not yet," Marigold said. She put her arm around my shoulder. "We're going to find him. Carver has a plan."

I beelined for Carver. He was in the kitchen holding a pendulum over a local map of Southill Village. "I'm trying a location spell," he explained. "Rowan got the map from a gas station. The spelling is accurate, up to a ten-mile radius. If I can get it to work, and they are somewhere in town, I should be able to pinpoint the exact location."

"What do you mean if?"

"I am having trouble connecting to him. Every time the spell tries to reach him, it's as if there's a negative reaction, and the pendulum stops cold on your house."

"Almost as if he were wearing a magic-repelling mojo bag?" I let out a blue streak of swear words that would've made a gnome blush. "Son-of-a-bitch. I gave Michael the bounce-bag before he left the house. Any spell you try to cast is going to come back at you."

Carver sighed and shook his head. "That's why it keeps pointing at your home on the map."

"Damn it!" I couldn't catch a single break.

Why, oh, why did I have to be such a helicopter mom? We could've found him if I had just trusted Michael to be all right and not given him the bag. This was my fault.

"Take it easy," Dahlia said. She picked Bob up from the floor and handed him to me. "Getting upset isn't going to help."

I set Bob down. Now was not the time for calm. It was time for the opposite of calm. "How are we going to find him?" Fair Konig flew past the kitchen window. "The pixies." Hope sprang eternal as I watched his blurry, razor-sharp wings carry him up. "Let Fair Konig in."

Rose, who wore a black nylon jacket with pink trim and black track pants as if she were ready to go for a run, got to the door first and flung it open.

"What is this excitement?" the pixie king asked. "Why is everyone here again? Do you need us for another spell?"

"Not another spell," I told him. "But do you still have some of your kin watching Michael?"

"The pixie vow!" Marigold exclaimed. She'd pulled her

glossy, dark brown hair back into a messy bun and wore a colorful caftan with a wide belt that fit her new half-giantess physique. "I'd forgotten about it."

"I have not," Fair Konig announced. "We have constantly surveilled Michael since the vow was made."

"And?" Carver, Keir, and Rowan said at almost the same time.

"Where is he?" I asked the pixie. "Where is Michael?"

"I don't know what the big—"

I cut him off. "Where?"

"He is at the house of the man he calls grandfather," Fair Konig said as if it were as plain as the nose on his face.

"Grandfather?" Rose's pale skin went even paler. "It can't be."

But in my heart, I knew it was true. Bogmall had said she would destroy everything and everyone I loved. "She's taken Michael to Dad's place." I staggered to the counter and gripped it with both hands. I couldn't breathe. I couldn't think. My mind and heart raced at all the possible horrific outcomes.

"She's hyperventilating," I heard Rowan say in the distance. "Someone find a bag."

The kitchen began to spin. I fought to keep upright.

Iris, a woman's voice, said in my head.

I ignored her as I tried to regain control of my traitorous body.

Iris! she shouted my name like a demand.

What! I shouted back.

You can't win a fight you've already lost in your head. This isn't helping Michael.

I don't know what to do.

Yes, you do. Face your fear and fight.

"Never mind," Rowan said. "Her breathing is coming back to normal."

I felt a hand on my back, and then I was sitting in a chair with my head down. "You're okay," Keir said. "You're okay."

"Nothing's okay," I managed after a few seconds. "But it will be." I stood up and headed to the door.

"Where are you going?" Marigold asked.

"To exchange me for Michael and Dad. I won't let them get hurt because of me."

Dahlia got to the door ahead of me, her blue-green eyes staring me down as she blocked the way. "You've never been a stupid woman, Iris. Don't start now. Think about what you're doing. You can't go up there without a plan."

"How can you say that to me? If Dad—" My stomach lurched at the idea that my father might already be dead. "If she—"

"Fair Konig," Keir said. "Can your scouts get close enough to see what's happening without being detected?"

The pixie king nodded his affirmative. "We shan't fail."

Lu came into the kitchen. "We need a place to set up close to your father's but not so close that Bogmall will know we're there."

Rose perked up. "Like a base of operations!"

"Exactly like that," Lu confirmed. "We'll need a place that gives us a tactical edge, with tree coverage and a higher vantage."

"Higher vantage?" Rowan asked.

"I am an expert with a long-range rifle," she said. "Sometimes the simplest solutions work. Our best shot might be me taking my best shot."

"There's the old Smith place up on the hill above Dad's house. It's a shack now. No one has lived up there in decades."

Marigold said, "We used to play there all the time when we were kids. It was our kids-only fort when we were growing up. We still probably have some buried treasure up there."

"My jacks," Dahlia said.

Rowan nodded. "My Hot Wheels Sting Rod."

As much as I loved my siblings, we didn't have time for this walk down memory lane. "I agree with Rowan. The Smith place is a good location. We could see our house from there, so we always knew when Mom was looking for us. There's a crop of trees that gives the place some cover as well."

"Great," Lu said. "If you tell me how to get there, I'll go up now and set up a sniper station." She put her hand on my shoulder. "If I get a clear shot, I'll take her out. That's a promise."

Keir and I knew something about our enemy that the others didn't, and I worried it would be a real problem. "Bogmall wasn't born. She was created." Ms. Alexander had said that Bogmall should've died after a few months. The fact that she hadn't worried me. "I'm not sure she can be killed with conventional weapons."

Lu gave me a cocked head stare. "I sure would love a chance to test the theory, though."

"Created how?" Carver asked.

"She was a clay baby." The idea was stranger than any fiction I'd ever read. "My mother had her sculpted and brought to life to fool Derrick Asher into thinking the child was me. She'd never planned for the creation to survive."

Carver swore under his breath.

"You've heard of this before?" Keir asked him. "The closest I've ever read about is the Jewish golem, but golems aren't people. They do their creator's bidding, but they don't have minds of their own."

"We know that's not Bogmall." I shook my head. "She's her own master."

"I think you're right, Iris." Carver sat on the arm of the sofa and sagged as if the weight of the world was on his back. "I'm not sure she can be killed."

Well, that was terrible news. "Why?"

"A clay baby isn't fashioned to create humans. They were vessels for the spirits of fallen gods. If you're right and Bogmall is one of these creations, then—"

"Then we're facing another god," Keir finished.

Carver nodded. "Or at least a demi-god."

Why did it always have to be gods? There were whole-ass grown people walking around in this world who never had to even meet a god, let alone have to face one down in battle.

"I still vote for shooting her in the head," Lu said. "If nothing else, it will make me feel better."

I agreed with her. "What else do you know?" I asked Carver.

"Even if we destroy her body. She's immortal. She'll find another body."

I thought about all my encounters with Bogmall and her desperate need to claim power she didn't possess. "She doesn't know," I muttered.

"What?" Keir asked.

I looked at him and repeated, "She doesn't know. She thinks she's a person. She believes she's my sister, born out of the same womb. She doesn't know she's immortal." I put my cool palms against my hot forehead. "If Bogmall knew she was god-made, she wouldn't be trying so hard to best me all the time. She's doing everything she can to become more powerful than me. To prove she's better than I am. Her vendetta is in thinking that I'm the favorite, and she's the spurned child."

Dahlia nodded eagerly and automatically went into psychiatrist mode. "Abandoned child syndrome, more correctly called CEN, Childhood Emotional Neglect. Without psychiatric help, these children can develop maladaptive behaviors."

"If by maladaptive you mean killing witches and snorting their magic like Tony Montana on a coke binge?" I gave my oldest sister a "seriously?" look. "Then, yeah, she's seriously maladaptive."

"How does this help us?" Rowan asked. "She's still immortal."

"Right," I agreed. "But she doesn't know she is. Which means she's still acting like someone with some-thing to lose. That's our advantage."

"It doesn't sound like much of an advantage," Rose commented.

I stretched my neck, and it gave three loud cracks. I felt as if I hadn't slept in weeks, and the strain on my body was taking a toll. "But as Dad likes to say, it's better than a sharp stick in the eye."

Fair Konig was back, and he waved urgently. Rose let him back inside. "The son and grandfather are tied up in the basement. In the living room, there are two identical versions of the boy's father. One with bruises and one without, then one of the versions became a blonde woman."

So Bogmall hadn't possessed Evan. She'd dopple-ganged him. How? Who knew? She'd been growing in her powers, the same as me. I had no idea what she was capable of at that point, so I had to be ready for whatever she threw at me.

"Is the bruised one okay?"

"He is unconscious. It is hard to tell without getting closer."

"Don't risk it," I told him. "Thank you, Fair Konig." It was some relief to know that Michael and Dad were alive and kicking. What was she planning?

Rose zipped her jacket closed. "I'll guide Lu to the Smith house so she can get her sniper stuff going."

"Rose," I chided. "You're pregnant. The last place you need to be is in the middle of all this."

"She has my father and my nephew," my youngest sister snapped. "If you think I'm staying out of this fight, you've got another thing coming."

Lu said, "She can be my spotter. She'll be far away from the action but still contributing."

"Fine." I was too tired to fight my family. Not when I had to prepare for the biggest battle of my life. "Don't shoot the real Evan," I added, just in case Bogmall morphed into him again.

"I'll try not to."

"There is no try," I told her. "Only do."

She crossed her eyes at me. "Okay, Yoda."

"I can make more mojo bags," Carver contributed. "It would give everyone at least some protection from Bogmall."

"Thank you," I told him, grateful for the eclectic witch's help. "Everyone keep in mind that the blonde bitch isn't above good old-fashioned murder. She straight-up stabbed Derrick Asher, and she liked it. A lot. Her magic isn't the only thing that makes her dangerous."

Zev, who had quietly watched the drama unfold, leaned his hip against the kitchen sink. "If we cannot kill her, there may be a way to trap her spirit and render her impotent."

"How?" I got up and faced him. "How do we trap her?"

"Using your anima and my fire," he replied.

"Zev, no," Marigold whispered.

"Your fire?" I asked. "I thought it hadn't returned."

"I can feel it just below the surface of my skin, but I've fought the returning to keep it away." He gave my sister a meaningful look. "If I accept my flame, I won't be able to put it back in the bottle."

In other words, he wouldn't be able to be with Marigold anymore.

My sister's lip quivered as her eyes glittered with tears. "If it has to be done to save my dad and Michael, then it has to be done." I could hear the cost in every word. Zev was the love of her life, and she was willing to give him up to save the lives of her family.

"No," I said. "There has to be another way. Besides, I've just sparked to anima. I don't even know if I could fulfill my part."

Zev's expression was impassive. "It is simply a matter of removing her soul and putting it in a clay vessel, much like your mother did when she created Bogmall."

"Wow, easy-peasy," I replied. "Seriously? Unless there is a 'Soul Removal For Dummies' handbook, I don't think this will work."

"I have seen you do great things, *sahira*." He narrowed his amber gaze at me. "Terrible, miraculous things. You will put her soul into a vessel, and I will seal it shut."

"If you can seal it with fire, why can't I? I have ignis-craft at my fingertips." And since I'd eaten Volres and vomited him, it had become my most effortless magic to wield. "Just tell me what I need to do."

"It has to be ifrit fire," Zev said cooly. "It's the only way."

"How do you know this?"

He grimaced, the first sign of emotion since my sister had given him the green light. "I know this because it is the only way to imprison a djinn."

CHAPTER 19

MY HEART BROKE AS I WATCHED ZEV AND MARIGOLD from my kitchen window. They'd gone out to the garden to speak privately. She and Zev had been inseparable since Iron Grove. I hated that their happiness had been so brief. Guilt and shame joined rage and fear. If I hadn't hated Bogmall already, this would've sealed the deal.

Keir, Rowan, and Dahlia had split up to search local stores for clay that had a high aluminum and silica count. According to Zev, the clay needed a high melting point to make the vessel strong enough to hold Bogmall's spirit. Linda would've simply pulled it from the ground. Damn it, I missed my gnome!

I practiced on some modeling clay I'd found in the hall closet. It had been left over from a school project from Michael's eighth-grade year. He'd had to make a solar system model. Michael had waited until the night before it was due to tell me about it. I'd spent the entire night forming planets to revolve around his cardboard sun. The clay was old and hard, but I made it work. I worked the colorful material with my hands to get it soft, then reached into the dough with my tera-craft.

I'd looked up various kinds of trap jars on my phone, and I found a variety of ancient djinn jars that had faces carved into them and sealing symbols carved into the lids. Zev told me I didn't have to get fancy and to keep it simple to prevent weak spots. His fire was stone melting hot, and he would seal the jar and harden it around Bogmall when I got her inside the vessel. It was a very optimistic plan, one that I had my doubts about based on my lack of ability. At this point, Bogmall had left me with little choice but to try.

"Flex and fold, bend and roll." I moved my fingers around the clay and watched with satisfaction as it began to take shape. I'd been at tera-craft the longest, so it only took three tries to form a simple receptacle that reminded me of the ancient Egyptian canopic jars. "What do you think?" I asked Carver.

He'd been working hard to get the mojo bags ready, along with making a few weaponized charms as well. He looked up from the task and nodded. "Good. It looks canopic."

"That's what I thought," I said. "I edited an art text-book a couple of years ago, and it was illustrated. Some of the jars were pretty ornate, but others were plain, like this one. Still, I'm happy with it." I looked at the clock. It was after six and starting to get dark. We planned to go at night for tactical reasons. Even so, I was anxious to get going.

"Would you happen to have a scrying mirror?"

"I have an obsidian mirror compact," Carver said. "It's light and travel's well."

"Can I use it?"

"Certainly. I'll get it from my kit." He grabbed his bag from the living room and brought it into the kitchen. "What are you planning?"

"I don't know," I said. "I'm hoping I can talk to Bob." As if hearing his name, the big floofy muffin of love rubbed his head against my hand. I gave him a wan smile. "There you are." I focused back on Carver. "He's my spirit guardian, but it's difficult to get guidance from him when he's here. If I'm going to try and move a soul, I'll need a little direction."

His interest was piqued. "Do you think it will work?" He opened a flap on the side of his kit and took out what looked like a folded piece of gray canvas. "It's an oilcloth," he said as if reading my thoughts. "A cotton weave coated with linseed oil. It makes it waterproof, and linseed has natural properties to help keep demons and other spirits from coming through the mirror without my permission."

Was that why there was a blue cloth over Bob's mirror? "So, I'm hearing you say, don't leave it uncovered when unattended."

Carver nodded. "Lesson number one."

"What's lesson two?"

"Don't follow any rabbits through the looking glass."

His tone was teasing, but I could tell he was serious. "Follow how?"

"It's tempting to reach out to the people we have loved and lost, but you must be careful not to join them.

The living can't occupy the world of the dead for long without becoming one of them."

"Got it. No visiting dead friends or relatives. Any other words of wisdom?"

He shrugged as he unfolded the cloth and handed me the mirror. "See what you can do."

The obsidian compact looked the way it sounded. It reminded me of a makeup compact that had powder and a mirror. Only there was no powder inside, and the mirror was a highly polished circle of obsidian stone. I picked up my beautiful Bob and said, "what say you, dude? Can you go back to your world and see if we can visit through the mirrors?"

Bob's purring ramped up, and after a quick nuzzle, he disappeared.

"I guess that's a yes," Carver said.

I placed the mirror on the table and stared down at it.

"What are you doing?"

"Bob said I have to look past what's there and see what I don't expect."

"Makes it a little hard to find the things you want," Carver commented.

"Tis true, Carver dude." A shadow figure appeared on the obsidian surface. "But it makes it easier to find what you need."

"Bob!" It worked. I could see and talk to him. "It's so good to hear your voice."

"Our time is short, fair, Iris. You must make haste."

"You've heard the plan. Will it work?"

"It either will," he said with too much Zen. "Or it won't. But I believe you will be triumphant."

"How do I move a soul?" I asked him. "How do I remove it from her body?"

"The same way you removed your own," he said simply.

"How did I do that?"

"I don't know." Bob spread his dark arms apart. "But you do. The knowledge is there. You just have to figure it out."

Just once, I'd like one of my guardians to be like, place A into B, circle C, and say Boo on D. Straight forward and no bullshit instructions. "Thanks, Bob."

He nodded. "I am glad to have formally met you, Iris Everlee." He bowed. "I'm proud to be your Boopalicious Butter Muffin." The obsidian went clear as Bob disappeared.

"That was enlightening," Carver said. "I feel lucky to have been blessed to guide you, Iris. You are a gift."

"Thanks," I said wearily. "I don't feel like a gift."

"True gifts never do." He gave me a strange look and then leaned in close. "I know this is not the time, but can I ask a personal question?"

"It depends on how personal," I said. "If you want to know my age, sure thing. If it's my weight, you can go to hell."

He chuckled. "None of that. It's about your brother."

"Okay...shoot."

"Is he seeing anyone?"

I raised my brows. "I don't know, but it doesn't hurt anyone to ask."

Keir, Dahlia, and Rowan returned with supplies.

"I got ball clay, porcelain, and something called fire clay," Keir said.

"I came up empty," Rowan admitted. "I couldn't find a store in town that carried anything other than modeling clay. I was glad when Keir called to let me know I could end the hunt."

I looked at Dahlia. "What about you?"

"I found silica at the garden store. I grabbed it just in case." She gestured with her chin toward Keir. "I was glad I could stop searching too. This town needs more stores."

"Where did you find all that?" I asked Keir.

"At the college. I stole it from the supply room in the art department."

I grinned. "Diabolical."

"Genius," Dahlia approved. "I wish I would've thought of it."

Zev came back inside without Marigold. "She wants a moment alone," he explained.

"Is she okay?" I asked.

"No." He didn't expand on the answer. He didn't have to.

"Are you?"

"No." He looked at my vessel and cocked his head to the side. "It looks like a canopic jar."

"Then I did it right."

He shook his head. "The opening must be a narrow stem and the belly round. That will hold the spirit securely in place." He examined the clay Keir brought and the silica powder Dahlia had in a bag. "The fire clay mixed with silica will be sufficient."

"I'm glad you approve."

"The instant you get her soul in the bottle, I will use my fire to seal the lid and harden the clay until there is no escape for her."

"Got it, bottle and seal."

He narrowed his gaze at me. "For what I am giving up, we cannot fail."

His words were a gut punch of pressure. "I—"

"I'll meet you there, *sahira*. I will be ready." He blinked his eyes and vanished from the kitchen.

"I don't think he wants to talk about it," Rowan said.

"I think you're right."

Rowan moved to the other side of the table and began asking Carver about the ingredients in the charms. Carver, with the patience of a teacher, methodically went through each one. What it was, what it was used for, and how the combination worked together. At one point, I locked gazes with Rowan and gave him the "okay, I see you" nod. He gave me back the "I have no idea what you're talking about" head dip.

I picked the box of fire clay up and opened it. I had one shot at getting this right, and I prayed that Zev and Marigold's sacrifice would count. Bogmall was always a step ahead of me. Was this another trap? Would tonight be the night that she won?

Hell, no. I was going to send her straight to spirit prison with no chance of parole.

CHAPTER 20

WITH LUANNE AND ROSE SET UP ON THE SMITH property, Fair Konig's pixies were in constant contact with them through an old-fashioned relay, and we were getting real-time updates. So, when my phone rang at seven, and Michael's name appeared on my screen, I knew it wasn't him.

"Michael?" I answered. "Where are you? I've been worried. I haven't been able to get a hold of you or your dad since you left this afternoon." I hoped I sounded convincing. Worried, but not scared.

"Mom," he said. "I need you to come and get me. Dad lost it about the magic today, and I'm afraid he's going to do something extreme."

Goddess, the person on the other end sounded exactly like Michael, and my whole body shook."

"Tell me where you are."

"At Grandpa's house. I talked him into bringing me here, but now he's got a gun. He's gone mad. Over the edge."

It's not real, I reminded myself. I looked at Keir, who was on the phone with Rose. He mouthed the words, "Not Michael."

I nodded. "I'm coming to get you," I told Bogmall, working hard to keep the threat out of my voice. "Just hold tight. I'll make everything right."

"Thanks, Mom. I knew I could count on you." The phone clicked, and Bogmall, posing as my son, was disconnected.

"That bitch," I seethed. I smashed the canopic jar I'd made earlier, and it made a satisfying splat. "She's messing with me."

"Yes, she is," Dahlia agreed. "What's the plan?"

"You know you can't come with me, right? I need you and Rowan to stay with Marigold. Tonight will be especially hard, and I don't want her to be alone." It was a sound excuse. One I'd been preparing for all night. It was bad enough that Rose was at the Smith place, but at least she had Lu protecting her. I couldn't keep the others safe. I could barely keep myself safe. Besides, all my energy needed to be focused on one goal. Taking Bogmall out and saving my son, dad, and ex-husband.

"No," my eldest sister said. "We won't let you go this alone."

I pivoted my gaze to Keir, fighting the overwhelming feeling of gratitude. "I won't be alone." I looked at Carver. "Will you stay with them? Everyone gets a mojo bag. Bogmall is unpredictable. If she gets away from me, I want you to protect them if you can. Everyone at my dad's house and in mine are the most important people in my life. I won't be able to do this if I have to split my worries."

"What about the defensive charms?" he asked.

"Those were always for you." I touched his face. "Thank you for being my guardian."

"It's not over," he said.

I nodded and forced a smile. "Not by a long shot." Although, in my estimation, a long shot was all we were getting.

"Fine," Dahlia grudgingly conceded. "But I expect Rose to give us constant updates."

Impulsively, I hugged her. "I love you, Dahlia."

She stiffened for a split second, then relaxed. "I love you, too. Be safe. Kick ass."

"All those things," I agreed. "I'll do all those things."

Rowan didn't wait for me to come around the table. As soon as I let Dahlia go, he hugged me. "Stay safe, sis. Try not to die."

"Wise words," I replied. "I will *try* to live by them."

"Har, har," he said. "Love you."

"Love you back."

I reached back and took Kier's hand. "Ready?"

His mouth was set in a grim line. "Let's go."

Keir carried the clay vessel to the car. Marigold came running from the backyard. At over six feet tall, she lifted me from the pavement and hugged me until I felt my spine crack. "You get everyone home alive," she said. I could feel her tears on my cheek. "This isn't your fault. I wanted you to know. I don't blame you. It's Bogmall's. She's the only one to blame."

"I love you, Marigold."

"I know. I love you." She set me down. "Bring them home."

I nodded and wiped at my own tears. "I will." I hoped I wasn't lying.

BOGMALL HADN'T SAID to come alone, so bringing Keir wouldn't look suspicious. She probably even suspected that I would. Had she shifted back into Evan's form? Could she make herself look like Dad or Michael? The possibilities knotted my guts. With every kill, Bogmall got stronger and more unpredictable. If she wasn't such an evil bitch, I'd almost feel sorry for her. I couldn't imagine what it would be like to never feel like I was good enough or that I was unloved. On top of that, Asher's obsession with me must've felt like a punch in the teeth. She hadn't been the one he wanted. It didn't matter if the only reason he'd wanted me was to take my magic. I'd taken Daddy's attention, and like a toddler with an old toy, she'd wanted it back.

Of course, she was a toddler with god-like powers. That was a messy combination.

I had a knife strapped on that Lu had given me and a new bounce-bag from Carver. On top of that, the vessel was ready to go. I was anxious to get inside. I had to see for myself that Michael and my dad were okay. And I would do my best for Evan as well, regardless of our past.

My goal was to get my family free, no matter the cost to me.

Keir slowed down about a half mile from Dad's house

and pulled over to the side of the road. He stared at me for a moment, then kissed me as if I were the last drop of water in the desert. I gave into the moment and kissed him back with the same fervor. I was surprised when he said, "Marry me."

"What? Now?"

"After," he told me. "We take care of Bogmall, save the family, and then we get married."

"Are you trying to give me a reason to live?"

A smile tugged at his lips. "Is it working?"

"Yes," I said and kissed him again.

"Wait? Was that a yes, it's working, or a yes, you'll marry me?"

I shook my head and grinned. "Yes. It's a yes to both."

He wrapped his arms around me. "I love you, Iris Everlee. I'm so in love with you, it's embarrassing," he said, giving my words back to me. "I've loved you my whole life, and I'll work every day to show you how much."

"You had me at marry me," I told him. "I've never been loved so well."

He let out a quick breath and sat back in his seat. "Good. Now that's settled. Let's go get our boy. And your dad. Evan, too, if possible."

"Keir!"

"Kidding," he said. "Sort of." He put the car in drive. "Don't die, okay."

"Back at you."

We were in Dad's driveway a minute later. Keir was in charge of keeping the vessel safe, which was probably a good idea. I was a klutz from way back. Chances were good, I'd trip on air and drop the djinn jar. That would turn our long shot into a no-shot.

He had put the jar in a bag like he was carrying groceries, and I led us up the ramp to the front porch. Taking a deep breath, I thought, okay, here goes everything.

I knocked, something I wouldn't normally do, and cussed myself for not just walking inside. I opened the door. "Dad? Michael? Anyone home? I'm here."

Michael came around the corner, his dimples deep as he smiled.

I looked around the living room. "Where's your dad?"

"He left," Michael said. "I talked him down and told him that you were on the way. He couldn't get away fast enough."

"Uh-huh. And your grandfather?"

"Oh, he's working in the basement," he said. He saw Keir behind me. "I'm glad you came," he told him. "It's nice to know you're there for me."

Keir forced a smile as he set the paper bag with the vessel by the coat rack. "Sure. I'm here for you."

This wasn't Michael, but I needed to be sure. "I'm sorry if your dad scared you. We'll get you home so you can play some Call of the Mandrakkan with Darren."

"Sounds good," he said. "I'm ready to go."

"I'm sure you are." Michael's friend was Doug, and they were playing Call of the Siren Stormers. I'd made up the word Mandrakkan. My son would've corrected me on both counts. This was not my son. I glanced at Keir. "You should go say hi to Dad. Tell him the good news."

"What news is that?" Bog-Michael asked.

"Keir and I got engaged." I couldn't stop the smile of triumph on my lips as her lip curled into a sneer.

"Congrats, Mom," she said. "Keir." Bogmall had already intimated that she'd believed Keir should be hers. Keir had been born seconds before me, and when I took my first breath, he'd bonded with me in a rare linking that only happens once in a millennium. It could be artificially forged the way Thomas and Freya were linked, but what Keir and I had was destiny, pure and simple. It was something Bogmall would never experience, even if she managed to kill me.

Bog-Michael nodded as Keir walked past her to the basement stairs. Why hadn't she stopped him? Last we'd heard, Dad and Michael were both downstairs, still. Maybe she'd wanted me alone. Well, here I was. Why wasn't she attacking me? Her end game was to see me decimated.

I gave her a tight smile. "Thanks, babe. I know how happy you are for us."

"Definitely." She hadn't moved from her location across the living room, and I wondered if it was on purpose. I was still at the door. Did she want me further in? She'd let Keir go to the basement without any argument. The fact that he hadn't come back made me nervous.

I slipped my hand into my pocket, rolling the bounce-bag between my fingers. "I'll get Keir, and we can go."

"I'll come with you." Bog-Michael gestured toward the basement.

I strolled across the room, trying not to raise suspicion. Bogmall could possess people, and now she could transform into the likeness of other people as well, which begged the question. Was this a shapeshifted Bogmall or possessed Michael? The way I fought her would depend on the answer.

Time to find out.

I crossed the room with more confidence than I felt. "What's that on your shirt?" I reached out and pulled the old trick of touching Michael's chest, and then at the last minute, when his head was tilted down, I shoved as much power into my hand as possible, earth, water, air, and fire, then moved my hand up and booped her nose as I unleashed just the barest spark.

"Made you look," I told Bog-Michael.

"What was that?" she asked as the mask she wore began to ripple.

"I'm just playing, kiddo," I told her. "Like we always do." I mean, what did she know, right?

I knew Fair Konig's pixies were watching from a secure hiding place and that Lu was up on the hill with a sniper rifle pointed in our direction. A bullet might not kill the blonde bitch, but it could incapacitate her long enough for me to get her in the jar. I had to trust that Zev would come in time to seal the vessel shut.

Where was Keir? If this was a trap, why hadn't Bogmall sprung it? Or maybe she had, and I didn't know it. I followed her around the corner to the basement door.

The quiet made my stomach twist. "Dad? Keir?" I was still behind Bog-Michael, ready to move. Ready to fight.

Calm, Keir had taught me. Adrenaline will get you killed. I forced my breathing and my heart rate to slow enough to keep my thoughts clear. Panic was not my friend. Not in this case. I reached out with my elements, trying to discover what Bogmall was hiding. I hoped it wasn't Evan's dead body. The fact that she was acting as if he'd left didn't bode well for him. No matter how I'd felt now or in the past, I didn't want to see him harmed.

The only magic I could feel was coming from Bog-Michael. It pissed me off that she was wearing my son's visage like a costume. I picked at the threads of the spell that kept her appearance stabilized. *One, two, three,* I plucked. My eyes widened as Michael's image shimmered, and behind the façade, I saw Bogmall's smug face.

I waited for her reaction to my manipulation of her spell, but I quickly discovered that she had no idea. She continued as if she were still wearing a solid Michael suit.

I shifted my focus to look beyond as Bob had instructed when I'd looked into his mirror. *Look past what you see and think of home,* he'd told me. It wasn't the home part that was important. It was the looking past. You don't always see what you want, but you see what you need. That was the lesson of the scrying mirror.

I stopped and took the obsidian compact from my pocket, and flipped it open.

"Fixing your makeup?" Bogmall asked.

I held the compact up to my face and peered past my reflection to Bogmall's and frowned. Her skin was gray and sallow, and she looked nothing of the woman I knew. I could see fragmented pieces of yellow, green, and silver magic as if they were disintegrating. Was she becoming more powerful or more unstable? Maybe both.

"What are you waiting for?" she asked.

I put the obsidian away and faced her. "I could ask you the same thing." Quick and precise, I placed my hand on her chest. "*Spirit of divine, unwind and untwine. Quick and deft, a soul bereft, answer to me. I set you free.*"

Bogmall's eyes widened as she grasped my hand and tried to push me away. "What are you doing?"

I could feel needles of her magic flowing out of her body and into my hand.

"No," she shouted. "Stop."

I wouldn't. Not until I had her spirit locked away in a jar for all eternity. I was only going to get one chance, and I would make it count.

"*Spirit of divine, unwind and untwine. Quick and deft, a soul bereft, answer to me. I set you free,*" I incanted again. Bog-Michael's appearance began to melt and twist, and it reminded me of when the Nazis opened the Arc in the first Indiana Jones movie. "*Spirit of divine, unwind and untwine. Quick and deft, a soul bereft, answer to me. I set you free.*"

"Taranis," the creature called out to its god. "Do not forsake me!" Its voice became high-pitched and frantic as it struggled to free itself.

With a sickening gurgle, the body collapsed to the floor, and I watched in horror as the writing stopped and Redbeard was lying on the ground at my feet. I had his corrupt, broken spirit in my hand. But it wasn't the soul I needed. He'd been a pawn. Another trick in Bogmall's arsenal of tricks. She wasn't a shapeshifter. She'd cast an illusion spell, but she'd tied the spell so deeply to the man that it had become part of his flesh.

A cackle from the basement door brought me up

sharp. Bogmall had my son, the white bone knife pricking his throat as rivulets of blood streamed to his collar.

"Well, done, sister," she said. "You managed to surprise me." Keir was sprawled, unmoving, on the floor at the bottom step. "Now, it's my turn to surprise you."

Michael's eyes flashed with fear as she threw him down the steps.

She licked the tip of the knife and smiled as she sang, "Suuurpriiise."

CHAPTER 21

"You're fucking dead," I fumed, shaking off the rotted soul and gathering my fire. "I'm going to kill you."

Bogmall laughed. "Not if I kill you first."

I hurled a fireball at her at the same time she called out, "*Gale flatus!*"

The explosion of our two spells meeting threw me back into the living room. I scrambled to my feet. Made a brief apology to my childhood home and said, "splinter and poke, shooting shards I invoke." I grabbed the wooden floors with my earth magic, and when Bogmall reached the top stair, I shoved all my energy into turning the hall into one large shrapnel grenade. She stepped onto the floor, effectively pulling the pin. Wooden splinters the size of stakes sprayed in all directions.

I heaved a breath as the energy spent knocked me for a loop. My heart sank as Bogmall, looking like a human porcupine, walked of her own volition into the living room. Her face and body were covered in blood from her wounds, and I choked when she started pulling the bigger spikes out and throwing them to the floor.

"Is that all you have?" she asked. "I thought you were supposed to be *special*." The way she said special felt as if she'd been hearing the word used her whole life in connection to me.

"I'm not special," I told her. "I was just another prize to be used by Asher and his cult, same as you."

"We are not the same." Her menacing gaze bore into me. "It should've been me. If I had been born with your power, I would've had everything. You waste so much. You don't even understand the privilege and the might that comes with possessing all five elements. You are the rarest of tru-craft witches, and yet, you spend your days as a..." she spat the next word out. "Homemaker."

I worked from home, but even if I didn't, there was nothing wrong with wanting to take care of my family. "Wow, you really are a jealous bitch. If you knew anything at all, you'd know that family is where the greatest power lies." I thought of my siblings and the way they rallied for me when I needed their help, and my friends were always ready to take my side in a fight and made great sacrifices so that goodness could win. "You have no one," I said. "What you see as weakness is your own fragile ego unwilling to see that the only reason anyone would follow you is out of fear or for the power you offer. That's not real. You are not real."

Bogmall screamed like a banshee, shattering the windows behind me, then she threw herself at me, and we both went flying outside to the rough terrain that used to be my mom's garden. She used her magic to kick up a hail of dust and rocks, but when they reached me, the mojo bag kicked in, throwing her five feet back and landing her in a sprawl. I scrabbled to my feet. Earth, fire, air, water, I called upon them all to do my bidding. Large pointy rocks shot up from the ground around her, and my fire fused them into solid walls. Water gushed from the ground filling the basin, and I used air to close the lid.

When Bogmall didn't escape, I ran around the back to the kitchen door. I had to get to Michael and Keir. *Please, please,* I begged the goddess. *Let them be alive. Please, be alive.*

The ground opened in front of me, and Bogmall rose from the dust the way a phoenix rose from the ashes. Her eyes glowed white, and she bared her teeth. If the pixies were near, I needed them to get a message to Lu.

"For Lu. Michael and Keir are in the basement. They need help. Someone get to the basement!"

Bogmall laughed at me. "You don't get it." She shook her head as she floated across the ground in my direction. "You're dead," she said with great calm. "You're all dead. Nothing you do can prevent it."

It wasn't going to stop me from trying. I threw fire, hail the size of golf balls, and every rock in a thirty-foot radius at the out-of-control sorceress.

When she discovered that magic directed at me ricocheted back to her, she started blasting the ground around me. The garden took all punishment, but I was definitely getting hit in the process.

I don't know how long we were going at it, switching between defensive and offensive magic, never getting close enough to each other for non-magic means. Until a stone, the size of an apple smashed into my jaw and knocked me to the ground.

Fuck!

Bogmall flew at me, landing on top of my chest. She had her bone knife in hand. "I will take you so slowly you will beg me to get it over with."

"Why do you have to be so creepy?" I slid the knife Lu gave me out of its sheath and stabbed it into Bogmall's side. She arched up and howled. Dried blood flaked from her face and arms, making her look like the clay she'd been created from.

Her hands went to my neck. The knife scraped my cheek. "Goodbye, sister."

"We're not sisters," I said. "You're not my sister."

"I know the tale of our birth better than you."

"You've been lied to," I gritted. "Lied to your whole life. You're not a person. You're not human."

She didn't let go, but the knife came off my skin. "What kind of ploy is this, Iris? Do you expect me to fall for a tall tale from a desperate woman?"

"It's not a tale. It's the truth." I stared her in the eyes. "You can see if I'm lying or not. You are not my sister. You weren't even supposed to live. You're a decoy. No better than the clay ducks on a pond. You were made to fool Asher into thinking I was dead so he'd stop looking. My mother only had one child. Me."

The story had distracted Bogmall enough for me to get in one good blast of fire. She rolled off me, patting the flames eating her hair.

As I bear-crawled toward the house, praying my family was safe. I saw one of the pixies waving me to come. I got up off my hands and sprinted in his direction.

I heard someone shout, "*custodia spiritus!*" and I hit the ground as a blast of blinding white light behind me lit up the entire yard.

I rolled to my back and saw Carver, Rowan, Dahlia, Marigold, and Rose standing outside the circle. They all began to chant, "*custodia spiritus!*" as the wall of light grew higher.

Bogmall screeched with fury and rage. She threw herself at the walls, but she couldn't break through the barrier. "Hurry! The charms will burn through soon," Carver bellowed. "The jar! Get the jar!"

Suddenly, Zev was next to Marigold. He held her hand as she continued the chant. My siblings. The bravest people I knew. I ran into the house and grabbed the bag with the djinn jar. Every part of me wanted to go to the basement, but if I didn't act now, all the effort of my coven would be for nothing, and then we would all be dead together.

I raced with the bag to the circle. If they could hold her, I could capture her spirit. We could do this, I thought, as hope renewed.

I tripped over an exposed root and smacked face down into the dirt. I felt the clay vessel shatter beneath me. "Are you kidding me?" I roared to the sky. The barrier was lowering. The charms were almost done. I had to do something, or Bogmall would end us all. I killed the volcano god by swallowing his essence. Could I do the same with Bogmall? Would it even work?

I didn't know, but we were out of options. I had to try.

I got up and bolted to the barrier, using aero-craft to vault me over the wall inside the cage with the enemy.

Her feral grin displayed her confidence. "You're a fool," she said.

"And this is what real power feels like," I told her as I gestured to my family. Their bravery, their willingness to sacrifice for each other, for me, our love, that was where true power lived.

Bogmall cursed as she launched herself at me. We landed in a heap. Gravel dug into my shoulders as I pressed my fingers hard into her flesh, trying to find her soul. A god's soul. I found it, but I also discovered something else during my exploration. Her entire body was earth. She was still made of clay. I kneaded and folded with my mind, shaping and reshaping.

Bogmall's eyes were wide with dread. "What are you doing to me?"

"I told you," I hissed. "You're not real." I winced as her face caved in on itself and her arms skewed back in unnatural positions. Her legs bent back and flat against her shoulders. I worked the clay, molding and refining it, forcing it to shrink until it was a jar with a round belly, a long neck, and a lid with a djinn symbol for soul prison on top.

The bottle danced in my hands as Bogmall's soul searched for an escape. I'd trapped it using the body it once called home, and it was angry.

I held it, crying as Zev carefully took the jar from me. I watched as blue flames from his hands encircled the jar, turning it a glowing white. After a few minutes, he stopped. "That will hold it until I can take her to the prison world."

"It's over?" I asked.

He nodded. "Yes, *sahira*, it is finished."

I got to my feet, stumbling toward the house. I saw my dad sitting on the ramp; Evan and Michael were on the other side of him, dazed but alive. Finally, I saw Lu dragging Keir out into the open. "Help," she cried. "Help me."

I faltered for half a second as the terror of losing him turned me inside out before making a mad dash for him. "Keir!" I dropped to my knees beside him. What had Bogmall done to him?

"He's not breathing, Iris," Lu said, her voice panicked. "I did CPR, but I can't get him back."

I tried to start his heart with my earth magic, but nothing happened. I breathed air magic into his lungs. Still, nothing. Lastly, I searched for his soul. A sob choked from my throat when I couldn't find it. "He's gone," I cried. "He's gone." My heart felt as if it were being shredded into a million pieces. I had always thought my life for Keir was strong, but not die for you, strong. I was wrong. At this moment, I wanted to join him. Our souls could streak together across the Amicaregnum sky as we moved to the afterlife.

Marigold, Dahlia, Rowan, and Rose crouched around me, their love forcing me away from the dark edge from where I teetered. "I can't...." I said. "I can't do this without him."

Then I heard the bronze lady's voice in my head.

. . .

*BLOOD OF MY BLOOD, **all is not lost.***

Tears of my tears, there is a cost.

Between life and death, I have walked the line. With obsidian, trade his soul for mine.

Summon strength from goodness and right and think of me when bathed in moonlight.

Goddess, bless thee.

MOTHER? I asked.

*I AM SO **proud of you, Iris. Goodbye for now, sweet child. We shall meet again.***

THEN SHE WAS GONE. I shook my siblings away and retrieved the mirror from my jacket and opened it up. I focused past what I could see and thought of Keir. I searched for our love, for the times we laughed, the times we fought for each other, and I remembered how the passion between us had only grown stronger.

Trade his soul for mine, she had said.

"I bargain for the spirit of Keir Quinn," I said aloud. "In trade for Heather Goodall."

The black glass rippled and swirled, and I saw his gray eyes staring at me through the obsidian. "There you are," I whispered. "Back to your body, you go."

Only when his soul settled back into his physical form and he gasped his first breath did I dare to live.

CHAPTER 22

A FEW DAYS LATER, KEIR HAD FULLY RECOVERED. Carver had discovered a residue spell designed to target my guy's puca. He hadn't been able to shift since the spell had killed him. It was a worry for another day. He was alive, and I was happy to spend the rest of my life with him, puca or not.

The next day, I took my grimoire to Briarberry Falls and read Persephone Alexander the names of my ancestors. *Aideen Magee, 1678. Clionna Doon, 1705. Siobhan Adrian, 1782. Mary Ann Langford, 1834. Brigit O'Malley, 1880. Mira Roberts, 1912* as a show of respect for the women who had blazed the trail before me.

Above my name, I wrote *Heather Goodall, 1983.*

My mother had been a powerful witch, and if it hadn't been for Derrick Asher, the grimoire would've found her first. She had earned a place of honor with my ancestors, and it felt right to share this moment with one person in the world who remembered loving her. She'd not only guided me as the bronze woman, but she had also sacrificed everything for me. I would never let myself forget her courage.

Against all odds, everyone I loved had survived. My father's house, on the other hand, was toast. Rowan moved him into his spare bedroom. With all of his recent health problems, I hoped Dad would decide to stay with him for a while.

Oh, and Goldie moved in with Rowan, too. I'm pretty sure she's unkillable after the Iron Grove witch trials, so bonus! Carver also decided to relocate to Southill Village. The fact that he's sweet on my brother and the feeling seems mutual is icing on the cake. He said he has a lot to learn from me, but I know that he's the one who will be teaching us. I'm happy Michael will get to learn about magic before he sparks. Hopefully, he can avoid all the troubles I've faced. Thankfully, Evan went home to St. Louis, no worse for wear. He'd been drugged by Redbeard and barely remembered the entire day. Yay.

Unfortunately, Zev hadn't come back after taking Bogmall away, but I hope he and Marigold find a way to be together someday. I'd put Keir on the task of researching to see if we can help reunite the lovers. I got my happy ending at their expense, and I will always be full of gratitude for them both.

But today was a special day of joy, no sorrow allowed, and I'd called my entire family to be witnesses.

"Okay, everyone. I think I'm ready to do this!" Bob had been by my side the entire process, either through the scrying mirror or snuggling his cute self into my lap. "Where's Keir?" I asked Marigold as she came into the kitchen.

"He's waiting out in the garden for you, silly. Where do you think he is?"

Nearly losing him had made me clingy. Luckily, he didn't seem to mind. I gathered my new creation I'd made from the leftover clay and carried it outside. Where my family and friends waited for me behind the new stone bench Rose and Lu had bought me to replace the one that I'd shattered. I set the sculpture on the ground next to it and took out a scrying mirror Carver had made for me.

I let out a tentative breath. "Let's do this." I opened the mirror and focused past what I saw and focused on what I wanted. What I needed, and that's when I saw the pink, broken blur. Her mouth was still moving as if cussing up a blue streak.

Holding her in my mind, I called to her spirit, "*Linda the gnome, delightful and bright, let go of the darkness, come into the light. I call you to me. Come get into your new body.*"

I got the idea after pulling Keir out that maybe I could do the same with Linda. I'd built her a new gnome body from fire clay, and Keir had taken it to the university to fire it in their kiln. It turned her into a gnome who would be able to withstand attack from any man or beast, including a snotgurgle. I'd given her a fresh pink coat, with a sage green hat and sage green pants. Her shirt was lemon yellow, and her winklepickers a shiny black. On top of all that, I gave her sparkling green eyes, cherubic cheeks, and a beard that would make her the envy of her donsy.

But only if it worked. Keir's miracle had required a sacrifice, but the fact that I could still find Linda after almost a week gave me hope she was only stuck and still alive.

I invoked the spell again. *"Linda the gnome, delightful and bright, let go of the darkness, come into the light. I call you to me. Come get into your new body."*

"Is it working?" Rowan asked. Dahlia and Rose shushed him.

Michael was fidgeting like an expectant father. This would be the first time he'd be able to see her animated.

"Come on, Linda," I coaxed. "Don't do me like this. Come get your body, girl."

I felt the thread of her energy connect to mine, and with the precision of someone who was the Classic Operation Game champion in eighth grade, I was confident I could thread this needle. For a moment, I held her warm spirit in my hand, and then, after giving thanks to the goddess, I released her into her new body.

I think we were all holding our breath, I know I was, as we waited a few seconds in painful silence to see if the spell would take. And then it happened.

Linda blinked.

"Oh, my gawd!" Michael jumped back with surprise as Linda beaned me right between the eyes with a pebble.

"Stupid, *Klienkind*," she berated me. "What took you so long?" She craned her head to look at her backside. "You could've given me a bigger keister."

I laughed as my brother and my sisters hugged each other. Keir wrapped his arms around me and kissed me stupid.

Linda looked at Michael, and I swear she teared up. "It's so nice to finally meet you, *Liebling*."

Michael smiled, his dimples deep and his eyes wide open for whatever came next.

I leaned into Keir's arms and happily sighed. Some people worry there's no life after forty, but I'm living proof that if you surround yourself with adventure and love, there is no greater age to be. In other words, it's all elemental.

The End

Coming Next in the Grimoires of a Middle-aged Witch Universe: **Burning Djinn of Fire**, a standalone novel featuring Marigold and Zev!

Marigold's love is a burning thing. And she'll face a fiery ring if that's what it takes to get him back!

PARANORMAL MYSTERIES & ROMANCES

BY RENEE GEORGE

Grimoires of a Middle-aged Witch
Earth Spells Are Easy (Book 1)
Spell On Fire (Book 2)
When the Spells Blows (Book 3)
Spell Over Troubled Water (Book 4)
Ghost in the Spell (Book 5)

Peculiar Mysteries & Romances
You've Got Tail (Book 1)
My Furry Valentine (Book 2)
Thank You For Not Shifting (Book 3)
My Hairy Halloween (Book 4)
In the Midnight Howl (Book 5)
Furred Lines (Book 6)
My Wolfy Wedding (Book 7)
Who Let The Wolves Out? (Book 8)
My Thanksgiving Faux Paw (Book 9)

Nora Black Midlife Psychic Mysteries

Sense & Scent Ability (Book 1)

For Whom the Smell Tolls (Book 2)

War of the Noses (Book 3)

Aroma With A View (Book 4)

Spice and Prejudice (Book 5)

Age of Inno-Scents (Book 6)

Aroma Holiday (Book 7)

Witchin' Impossible Paranormal Mysteries

Witchin' Impossible (Book 1)

Rogue Coven (Book 2)

Familiar Protocol (Booke 3)

Mr & Mrs. Shift (Book 4)

Barkside of the Moon Paranormal Mysteries

Pit Perfect Murder (Book 1)

Murder & The Money Pit (Book 2)

The Pit List Murders (Book 3)

Pit & Miss Murder (Book 4)

The Prune Pit Murder (Book 5)

Two Pits and A Little Murder (Book 6)

Pits and Pieces of Murder (Book 7)

Hex Drive

Hex Me, Baby, One More Time (Book 1)

Oops, I Hexed It Again (Book 2)

I Want Your Hex (Book 3)

Hex Me With Your Best Shot (Book 4)

Hex Me All Night Long (Book 5)

Madder Than Hell

Gone With The Minion (Book 1)

Devil On A Hot Tin Roof (Book 2)

A Street Car Named Demonic (Book 3)

SENSE AND SCENT ABILITY

A NORA BLACK MIDLIFE PSYCHIC MYSTERY BOOK 1

Chapter One

"I think I have a brain tumor," I blurted as I flung open my front door for my best friend, Gillian "Gilly" Martin. She held a bottle of wine in one hand and a grocery bag filled with honey buns, potato chips, salted nuts, and chocolate-covered raisins in her other.

"You don't have a brain tumor." Gilly passed off the bag and the bottle, then brushed past me, shrugging off her coat and hanging it on the hall tree. It had been a cold March, with temperatures in the low 40s most days. Under the coat, Gilly wore a form-fitting, long-sleeved, baby blue turtleneck sweater and black palazzo pants that flared out over a pair of black flats. Her straight chestnut-brown hair was in a loose ponytail for our girls' night in.

"Are you pooping okay?" she asked. "The doctor said you weren't supposed to strain. You could pop internal stitches."

"Quit asking me about my bowel habits," I said. "As of

193

yesterday, I've been cleared to resume normal activity. Like straining when I poop. Besides, I'm worried about my head, not my butt." After all, my mother had died of brain cancer. "I've been... " I trailed off, trying to find the right words. "Seeing things."

Gilly squeezed my shoulder in an effort to comfort me. "You had a hysterectomy, Nora. Didn't the doctor say you might feel strange for a while?"

Um...if strange included dying on the operating table and then discovering strong scent-induced hallucinations, then yeah. I felt strange. I mean if death was gonna bring me a gift, I would've liked something a lot more useful than the ability to smell other people's troubles.

How could I possibly explain my new weird ability to her? Well, obviously, I couldn't. It had been eight weeks since my surgery, and I still hadn't figured out a way to confide in Gilly.

"Nora?"

I sighed. "I need a drink." I lifted up the wine bottle. "Let me pop this sucker." Gilly still looked concerned, but I smiled and nodded toward the living room. "Be right there."

A few minutes later, I handed Gilly her glass of Cabernet Sauvignon and sat down next to her on the couch.

"You know, regular activities include sex," Gilly said with a little too much enthusiasm. She waggled her brows at me.

"Sex hasn't been a regular activity for me in a very long time." Two years to be exact. I wasn't a prude. It's just that there hadn't been a lot of opportunities. Between caring for my mother during the last stages of her illness and dealing with painful uterine fibroids, dating and sex were the last things I cared about.

"You are way too hot to be celibate."

"Sure." I patted my swelly-belly. "I've gained ten pounds in the last two months."

"You just had your guts cut out," she said with a fair amount of exasperation. Then she flashed me her signature Gilly Martin smile, and added, "Besides, men like women with curves."

I frowned and pinched some of my stomach fat. "It's too squishy to be a curve."

She laughed. "Girl. I got squishy curves all over." She rubbed her tummy. "Including my midsection." She fluffed her ponytail. "And I'm sexy as hell."

I grinned. "You certainly are." I had always lacked the confidence Gilly displayed about her looks and body. She wasn't wrong about her sex appeal. Men were drawn to her like bears to honey.

"Have I told you lately how happy I am that you're back in Garden Cove?"

I rolled my eyes then grinned. "All the time."

"I can't help it. I missed you when you lived in the city." Her sigh held a hint of sadness. "Though, I'm sorry for the reason you had to come home."

Last year, my mother's brain cancer had progressed to its final stage. My father had died ten years ago, and I was an only child. Mom only had me. So, I'd taken a compassionate leave of absence from work as a regional sales manager for a prominent health and beauty line to care for her. It had turned into an early retirement when my employer decided they wanted to keep my temporary replacement, a younger, more cutthroat version of myself. Thankfully, they'd offered me a generous severance package if I would go quietly, including covering medical insurance costs until I qualified for Medicare in fourteen years.

I'd accepted their offer. Spending time with Mom until her final moments had been a blessing. I didn't regret a minute of caring for her. Of course, from the hospice workers, the aides, the nurses, the volunteers who would sit with her while I shopped, and even the chaplain who brought her some spiritual comfort, I hadn't done it alone.

My mother had been the rock of our family, a major source of comfort and stability. When she got sick, she'd minimized the severity of her cancer because she hadn't wanted me to worry. Honestly, I'd believed she'd beat it. I'd never seen Mom not succeed when she put her mind to something. If only I had known how bad it really was, I would have come home sooner.

Reconnecting with Gilly had been one of the major bright spots since moving back to Garden Cove. We'd been inseparable during elementary and high school. She'd been the maid of honor at my wedding and had done the pub crawl up in the city with me when my divorce had finalized. I had been twenty-nine at the time. It was hard to believe that twenty-two years had passed since then. When I was in my teens, I couldn't wait for high school to be over so I could make my own life. Then in college, I couldn't wait to graduate so I could be married. Later, when my marriage fell apart, I couldn't wait to be out of it so I could move away from Garden Cove and start my career.

I'd spent so much time wishing my life away that I'd failed to really live in the moment. I didn't want to be that person anymore.

My whole life had been go-go-go, and I was ready for some slow-slow-slow.

I squeezed Gilly's hand. "I missed you, too. You know, it's not too late to quit your job and come work with me in the shop."

Gilly smiled. "I like running the spa at the Rose Palace Resort."

"I know you do." I didn't press her. We'd had this conversation a dozen times since I'd bought Tidwell's Diner and converted it into an apothecary, where I sold homemade beauty and aromatherapy products. I couldn't afford to pay her what she was worth, anyhow. But it didn't stop me from wishing we could spend more time together. I considered myself lucky that she'd had tonight free.

Gilly was a single mom to teenage twins, and the high school was out for their short spring break that would end on Monday and Tuesday thanks to snow days in January that they still had to make up. The kids were doing overnights at their friends, while Gilly had packed a bag to stay in my guest bedroom and leave for work in the morning from here. Hence the wine. "How are the kids doing?"

"Like they would tell me." Gilly snorted. "They're teenagers, so they share as little as possible. Marco seems to be doing okay. He's dating a girl a year older than him.

A senior. Can you believe it? I wouldn't have ever dated a younger boy in high school."

"Marco's a good-looking kid."

"He's only sixteen and just like his dad," Gilly agreed. "Oozing charm and confidence. Worries me sometimes."

"He's not anything like Gio," I assured her. Marco, while moody and temperamental at times, had a kind heart, unlike his father, who only cared about himself. The twins never saw their dad anymore, and that was on Giovanni Rossi. After the divorce, he took a head chef position at an Italian restaurant in Vegas. He used his work as a way to avoid parental responsibility. Too often, Gilly carried that burden of guilt, as if it was her fault Gio had abandoned his kids.

"What about Ari?" I asked.

"She made the honor roll." Gilly's daughter's full name was Ariana Luna Isabelle Rossi. A beautiful name, but she preferred Ari. The girl marched to the beat of her own drum, and I loved that about her. Where her mother was hyper-feminine in both hair and clothes, Ari wore her hair like James Dean, and her outfits tended to be androgynous. "She's so smart, but I can't help but worry about her. She's so damned quiet. How in the world did I, a woman who can't shut up, raise a daughter who doesn't like to talk?"

"You got me there," I said, offering a sly smirk.

"Nora!" She smacked my arm. "You're terrible."

"Ouch." I rubbed the spot and laughed. "I really am. Good for Ari, though," I said. "She's always been a smart cookie. And her drive and ambition to excel will take her places." I didn't have children by choice, but that hadn't stopped me from agreeing to be Marco and Ari's godmother. When I lived in the city, I'd sent the kids packages every year for birthdays and Christmas, but I hadn't spent a lot of time with them until I returned to Garden Cove. "She's going to be just fine, even if she didn't inherit her mother's gift of gab." I slung my arm around Gilly's shoulders and squeezed, careful not to jostle our wine glasses.

I caught the sweet scent of raspberries with notes of citrus and vanilla.

Blurry shapes form...a woman stands in front of a large man who towers over her. Faces are hazy. It appears as if they're both made of colored smoke.

"It's over, Lloyd."

I recognize Gilly's voice.

"Don't be that way, Gilly," the man cajoles. "I didn't mean anything by it."

Gilly's voice chokes. "I really like you, but I can't be with someone who would say those things. Especially about my daughter. Ari is a great kid."

She turns away from him and he grabs her arm. Gilly gasps as he yanks her against his body.

"We belong together." He manacles both her wrists with his large hands. "You have to give me another chance."

"Get your hands off me," she says, pain evident in her shaking voice.

"I'll never let you go." His menacing tone chills me to the bone. "Never."

"Hello." Gilly snapped her fingers in front of my face. "Earth to Nora."

"What?" I said, blinking at my friend.

Her brow furrowed. "Are you okay?"

"You're going to get grooves between your eyes if you don't stop worrying about me." Although, at this point, I had enough worry for the both of us." "How is it going with the new guy you're dating? Lloyd Briscoll, right?"

Gilly went pale and the wine glass in her hand trembled. I took it from her, then placed both of our glasses on the coffee table. "Gilly?"

"I'm fine," she said, her voice pitched to an unbelievably cheery tone. "Didn't you promise me a date with Mr. Darcy?"

I'd wanted to tell her about my scent-stimulated hallucinations, and maybe now was the time. This was the first...er, vision I'd had about my best friend. Still...what if I was wrong? If I really did have a brain tumor, and these experiences were a symptom of being sick, then it would be stupid to worry Gilly. Besides, if she thought I was nuts, she might decide to tie me up, throw me in the car, and take me to the nearest emergency room.

But her avoidance of my question, in addition to the vision, stirred a bad feeling in the pit of my stomach.

"Tell me what's going on," I said softly.

Gilly took a sudden interest in a loose stitch at the bottom of her sweater, tugging on it to avoid my gaze. "We broke up." She paused. "Correction. I broke up with him." Gilly pushed up the cuff of her sleeve and revealed finger-sized bruises on her wrist.

"He did this?" I asked. My stomach clenched. What I'd glimpsed of Gilly and Lloyd's interaction had been real. Holy crap. Without thinking, I asked, "Was it something to do with Ari?"

Gilly gave me a sharp look. "How did you..." She shook her head then nodded. "I overheard him laughing with some of his buddies in the security office." Her hands were shaking now, and there was anger in her voice. "They were talking about Ari." Her eyes narrowed as her ire surfaced. "He called Ari a freak, and some other unsavory slurs that I won't repeat, because she happens to wear her hair short and the way she dresses."

I took her hand and gave it a pat. "He's an asshole."

"I marched right into that room gave him the it's-not-me-it's-definitely-you speech. He grabbed me and told me we were done when he said we were done."

"Is that after he told you he'd never let you go?"

Gilly paled. "Yes. How did you know that?"

Alarm kicked my adrenaline in. I skipped her question and went right to the important part. "That's a threat, Gilly. You need to call the police."

"And tell them what? Who's going to believe Silly Gilly over the head of security for the Rose Palace? Lloyd is an ex-cop, and he still has a lot of friends on the force."

"Yeah? Well, so do I."

"You mean your ex-husband chief of police who you haven't spoken to in ten years? That guy?" Gilly scoffed. "Shawn Rafferty didn't like me when you two were married."

Shawn and I had divorced for a myriad of reasons, but mostly because he'd changed his mind about wanting kids. I had not. When we divorced, we split everything down the middle, and since we didn't have children and we were both just starting our lives, I didn't sue for alimony. I didn't want anything tying us together anymore. Not even a last name, so I took back my maiden name. And then poof, like magic, it had been as if the five years we were married and the four years we dated never existed.

But say what you want about my ex-husband, he's a good cop. And, yeah, a good person. He and his wife had sent a lovely spray of lilies for my mom's funeral, and Shawn had even stopped in at the visitation. Our conversation, the first one we'd had since my dad had died a decade ago, had been short but not unpleasant.

"Shawn will believe you." I clasped both of her hands and looked her in the eye. "Promise me you'll call the police if that son-of-a-bitch comes within fifty feet of you again."

"We both work at the Rose Palace. Our paths are bound to cross." Gilly blew out a breath. "But I'll do my best to avoid him."

I stared at her hard, my mouth set in a grim line.

She raised her hand as if taking an oath. "And I'll call the police if he attempts to even talk to me." She pushed my shoulder lightly. "Now, come on. I didn't come over here to lament my tragic taste in men. You promised me a night of binge-watching Jane Austen movies, good wine, and all the popcorn I can eat."

My smile felt tight. Gilly was an adult, and she'd been living her life just fine for many years without me telling her what to do. "You're absolutely right. Let's fill up these wine glasses, and I'll start the popcorn. You break out the goodies." Like a weirdo, I loved mixing chocolate-covered raisins in with my salty popcorn. Yum.

Twenty minutes later, we were sitting on my comfy couch with throw blankets over our legs, a large popcorn bowl between us and honey buns on the coffee table. Our wine glasses were full of Cabernet Sauvignon, and our undivided attention was on Mr. Darcy.

"Why can't real men be like him?" Gilly bemoaned after Darcy gave Elizabeth moon eyes.

"No, thank you," I told her. "I like the fantasy of Darcy, but he's judgy and bossy and arrogant. Give me a guy who is genuinely interested in my happiness, and not what he *thinks* will make me happy. That's the guy I'll spend the rest of my life with." Not that I thought such a man existed. I wasn't content exactly, but I was resigned to living out my life as a single woman. I glanced at Gilly. At least, I knew I'd never be alone. Not with friends like her in my life. I nudged her and smiled. "Even so, I'll happily root for Elizabeth Bennet to get her man."

"So, you are looking for a man," Gilly said triumphantly.

"You're the worst," I said.

Gilly made a kissy face in my direction. "Best Bitches Forever."

High-beam headlights glared through my living room window. I shielded my eyes and waited for them to go off. They didn't.

"Who is that?" Gilly asked. "Were you expecting anyone?"

"No. Just you." I got up and looked outside with Gilly right behind me.

"Oh. Oh, no," she hissed. "It's Lloyd."

"Go lock the front door," I said. When she didn't move, I said with more force, "Now!"

Gilly took off toward the front door, and I moved

quickly up the stairs to my bedroom, ignoring my creaky knees as I retrieved my gun case from my bedside table. My hands were trembling as I opened the case and grabbed my compact 9mm and a full clip of bullets. I loaded the gun while I returned to the front of the house.

It was dark outside. "Is he still out there?" I asked.

"Gilly!" I heard a man shout. "Gilly, come talk to me. I just want to talk. I'm sorry about earlier. I didn't mean it. I swear. I promise it won't happen again."

Gilly had her body pressed against the wall and out of sight. "I think he turned off the light so he could see inside," she said. "He won't stop calling for me."

"How did he know you were here?" An awful thought occurred to me. "The kids?"

"No," she said. "They're staying the night with friends." She shook her head. "I told him a couple of days ago that I was coming over here to celebrate your recovery." Her pitch went up a notch as tears flooded her eyes. "I'm so stupid."

"He's stupid. Not you."

"Gilly!" he bellowed. "Come out and talk to me. Don't make me come in there after you."

"That is just about enough." I loaded a round into the chamber of my pistol and stalked to the door. "Call the police," I said.

"I already did," she said. "What are you going to do?"

"I'm going to get that jerk off my property."

I unlocked and opened the front door, walking out with my weapon extended in front of me. The wind whipped my hair across my face, and I pushed it back with my free hand. I hadn't bothered to put on shoes, and the rough concrete from my walk bit into my socked feet. I ignored the discomfort as I took aim at the drunk in my driveway.

Lloyd, a tall man, handsome, even with a receding hairline, gave me a look of sheer incredulity. He wore a dark nylon jacket with a tear in the pocket, his cheek was red and swollen, and his lip was bleeding. I guessed this wasn't the first fight he'd started tonight.

"Get back in your car and leave, Lloyd. And stay away from Gilly," I said. "The police are on their way, and if you're gone before they get here, I won't file a complaint."

"You can't shoot me." He laughed. "Castle law means I have to be in the place you live. Otherwise, you'll go to jail for assault or attempted murder."

"The way I see it, I can shoot you, then Gilly and I can drag you into the house."

He walked up to me and pressed his chest against the barrel of my gun. "Go ahead, tough girl. Shoot me."

The sour scent of beer mixed with whiskey made my stomach roil.

I recognize his out-of-focus form before the reek of booze confirms it. "Bitch!" Lloyd yells. He grabs a red-haired woman, his hands encircling her throat. Like Lloyd, I can't make out her face, and with her knees buckled, I can't tell how tall or short she might be, but I can feel her desperation. She struggles to escape but he is too strong.

"Please," she whispers, barely audible. "You're...choking...me."

He throws her to the ground and straddles her, his thick hands squeezing her throat. But who's his victim? I'm helpless. She's dying. He's killing her.

I snapped out of it, full of rage. I lifted the 9mm

higher and aimed at Lloyd's head. Something in my eyes must have frightened him because he took several steps back.

Sirens sang out in the distance.

"Tick-tock," I said to Lloyd. "A smart man would already be in his car."

He scowled at me. "Crazy bitch." On that note, he jumped into his vehicle, started it up, and squealed his tires as he reversed out of the driveway.

Gilly came running outside clasping a butcher knife. "Oh my gosh, Nora. You're a freaking superhero."

"When the police arrive, I'm filing a report," I said, trying not to pass out.

She whipped the knife around in the air. "But you told Lloyd—"

"Gilly, stop waving that thing before you hurt yourself."

She blushed as she dropped her arm to her side. "I forgot I was holding it. What are we going to say to the police?"

"The truth. Lloyd Briscoll is a bad guy, Gilly. Like, really bad." I shivered as pieces of the vision played in my head. "He needs to be reported. And you need to show them your bruises. I have a feeling this man isn't going to leave you alone without encouragement."

Click Here to Keep Reading!

YOU'VE GOT TAIL

PECULIAR MYSTERIES & ROMANCES
BOOK 1

Chapter One

SOME PEOPLE JUMP into the deep end of the pool feet first, some head first, but I've always been a traditional belly-flopper. Splashy, messy, and usually painful. Which still didn't explain why I was sitting on the floor of a closed diner, nursing my bruised butt, not to mention my pride, and staring woefully at a naked unconscious man in the middle of Peculiar, Missouri.

My parents are crazy from way back. Maybe that's where I get it from. Seriously, who names a child Ambrosia Sunshine? Two hippies, that's who. They told me when I was old enough to resent the flower child name that they'd thought it was cool at the time, but I personally believe it was the result of one too many 'shrooms. As it is, I've been forced to sit through many painful renditions of "You Are My Sunshine." If I had a dead body for every time I was teased, well, let's just say I'd get an express pass to the electric chair. Although, if I got a sympathetic judge, he'd probably consider my lifetime served.

Maybe my parents' experimentation with drugs is what had made me psychic. (No, I didn't say psychotic. I said *psychic*.) On the other hand, it could also explain why I'm so bad at it.

My ability allows me glimpses, more like screenshots, of the past, present, and future. But, clearly, the visions have *not* been helpful over the years. And the side effects, sheesh. Most of the time I feel a little dizzy when they hit, but every once in a while, it's as if someone has taken a sledgehammer to the inside of my skull. Usually, I can feel one coming on; otherwise driving might be an issue. If only they made medic-alert bracelets for my type of ailment. It certainly hasn't been a gift.

That's why my friendship with Chavvah Trimmel is so important. We'd met at the community college in San Diego. She thought my name was weird and awesome all rolled up into a spring roll. After finding out her family's propensity for strange biblical names, I thought it was a bit of the pot calling the kettle rusty. Chavvah, or Chav, as she likes to be called, was my first best friend. And when she's around me, my psychic mojo kicks up twenty notches. It's as if I can tap into some kind of mystic hotline whenever she's near.

As a matter of fact, the last time I'd gotten a clear vision had been in my dining room back in California. Chav, who'd been renting my spare bedroom at the time, had just turned down the heat on the spaghetti sauce, and I was setting the table. We were having an "I finally dumped the cheating bastard" celebratory dinner. Did I mention I'm a bad psychic? So I hadn't a clue what I was walking in on when I caught my boyfriend of three years having sex with the skank waitress from the coffee shop. On my couch, no less. Jerk. I took his spare key and kicked his ass (and the couch) to the curb.

At dinner that night, when the vision hit me, I'd hit the ground, along with some clattering dishes. I saw a present moment of Chav's parents huddled together, debating whether to call her about her missing brother. Talk about being the bearer of bad news. I didn't blame her for not believing me at first, or the stunned look she gave me when she called her parents, and it turned out to be true. Her brother Judah had dropped off the map.

Chav flew back to Missouri the next day. After a year of searching for him, the local police had pretty much given up on Judah, but by that time, Chav had forgotten about the ocean and fallen in love with the little town of Peculiar. Hell, from her letters and phone calls, I'd kind of fallen in love with the place as well. She'd found a restaurant in the rural town, a real fixer-upper, for the two of us to run. A fifty-fifty partner split.

I wasn't supposed to leave California for another two weeks, and Chav had said she needed to talk to me "in person" before I made the trip, but the text I'd gotten from her had sent me packing in a hurry.

All it said was: *Sunny. I need u.*

After that, every call I'd made to Chav went straight to voice mail. Without any real plan, I jumped into my gas-guzzling Toyota 4X4, which I had purchased explicitly for the move. One thousand six hundred and sixty-two point four miles later, as I drove over a swinging bridge (the only way in and out, I soon discovered) into the quaint little town, my whole body heaved a sigh of relief. I felt strangely wonderful. It was as if someone unzipped my off-the-rack skin and fitted me with a tailored Sunny suit.

The town looked very similar to Mayberry from *The Andy Griffith Show*. Dirt streets, old fashioned shops and houses, white picket fences, and lots of Chevy and Ford pickup trucks. I was a little nervous when my GPS said, "You have arrived," right outside a two-story yellow building on the corner of Third Street and Main.

My heart pounded as I stood outside our restaurant for the first time. I'd always expected some kind of fanfare. Chav waiting to usher me into our future. She'd even named the restaurant for me. Sunny's Outlook. I'd blame allergies for my eyes watering at that moment, but I knew it was a mixture of happiness and sadness all rolled into one big bundle. This was *our* place. Mine and Chav's. And she'd done it up spectacularly.

I smiled at the brightly colored lettering. All the letters except the big O in Outlook were blue. The O was not an O at all, but a bright orange sun. If it was possible to feel both warm and cold at the same time, I accomplished it.

Where was Chav? I knew in my bones something was wrong. The year we'd spent apart had dulled my psychic ability toward her, so once again I had become inept with crazy flashes that didn't amount to much of anything.

I jiggled the door handle. It wasn't locked, so being the smart, city-savvy girl I am, I decided to let myself in. After all, I owned half the joint, so I wasn't trespassing.

Darkness enclosed the front room except a few areas illuminated by sunlight filtering into the two small windows near the ceiling. They were surrounded by open wooden shutters. Where were the large storefront windows? This place was more dive bar than restaurant. Strange decor choice but my concern for Chav kept me from imagining a complete makeover. I couldn't find a light switch around the door. I should have just gone back out to the truck for a flashlight, but I thought I saw a panel on the wall across the room, and frankly, it was sheer laziness that moved me forward.

I managed to maneuver around the counter, open the panel, and flicked several of the switches at once. The lights came on and when I stepped back to admire my new home lit up—it didn't look half bad; hardwood floors, cute little tables with black-and-white gingham cloth, and a couple of booths with the same checkered design on the benches.

And that's when it happened. My heel caught on something large, and I fell ass-backward to the ground. It didn't take more than a nanosecond to see that I'd tripped over a naked man passed out cold on the floor.

After a startled yelp, heart palpitations, and worry that he'd wake up at any moment and kill me, I reached over and touched him. Just his arm, mind you. He didn't move, but his skin felt warm, and his chest raised and lowered, so I didn't bother to check for a pulse.

Instead, I found myself staring...for several minutes. (Come on. He was naked and lying on his back. Who wouldn't stare?) Dark-brown hair populated his broad chest and led to a happy trail that, well, if the circumstances had been different would have made me very happy indeed. He had thickly muscled thighs and arms, and his face, except for the scruffy five o'clock shadow, looked as if it had been chiseled by Michelangelo. Imagine a better-looking Wolverine (Hugh Jackman's version), but much younger and with a burly lumberjack vibe, and coarse, medium-length walnut-brown hair.

I chewed my lower lip as I took my time pondering the situation—in other words, I wasn't ready to stop staring at the naked man. His hair was near the same hue of brown as my own, when it wasn't dyed blonde, which was never. And mine was shorter with a better haircut. I sighed with regret. I already missed my stylist in California.

Taking a deep breath, I counted backward from ten to pull myself out of the hormonal frenzy going on in my head. The man was hotter than a habanero, but I wasn't looking for a date. I smelled a pungent sweet scent I hadn't noticed before, but frankly I was surprised any of my senses still worked. It was whiskey. Some kind of blended version, if I had to guess.

Great. Just perfect. Burly Hugh looked more and more like a drunk who had crawled into the diner to sleep off a bender.

I found an empty spray bottle by the sink and filled it with water. Positioning myself on the opposite side of the checkout counter (just in case I needed to make a run for it), I leaned over the top and proceeded to spritz the unconscious man. The mist must have been too fine, because other than the rise and fall of his chest, he still didn't move.

Crawling farther up onto the counter, I stretched my arms over the other side, hovering just inches from his face. I pumped the trigger hard three or four times, then screamed and dropped the bottle when his hand shot up and grabbed my wrist. The Neanderthal yanked me completely over the top and onto his naked self. He growled— honest to goodness, I wouldn't lie about such a thing. He growled. The noise started in his chest. I know, because I could feel it in mine, which was now crushed against him.

Why hadn't I just left and called the police? It would have been the easy thing to do—the smart thing. His arms were squeezed tight around me, and I became acutely aware of his Mr. Happy pressing against the skin of my thigh.

His eyelids cracked a peep, then he narrowed his gaze. "Who are you?"

"I..." I should be the one asking the damn questions, but the only ones coming to mind were completely inappropriate. Like, where did he work out? How good looking were his parents to create such a fine specimen of man? And did he have a girlfriend?

There was a moment, a very weak moment on my part, where I began to lower my face to his, our lips only centimeters apart.

What the hell am I doing? Where was my head? He could be a serial killer, a rapist, or someone *really* bad, like an Amway salesman. I turned my head away from his.

"Could you let me up, please?"

He squeezed me tighter. "Are you going to answer me?"

Finally, I gulped and squeaked out, "Sunny Haddock."

His left eyebrow rose. "Sunny Haddock?"

"Uh, that would be me. Yes." I'd been in town less than an hour and I was already famous. Well, my name was on the side of the building. "And you would be?"

"Babel Trimmel."

"Chav's baby brother?" I'd heard stories about him, but I'd imagined him to be terminally twelve. The age he'd been when Chav had left Missouri for the West Coast.

"Chavvie made a big mistake. She shouldn't have asked you out here."

Talk about judging someone before you get the know them. Barely through introductions and he already wanted me out. I've made a bad first impression before, but what the fuck? What didn't he like about me? Although maybe it wasn't about like. Because, by the rise of his hoo-ha against my leg, I could swear he liked me a little.

An unfamiliar flutter twittered in my stomach. It'd been awhile since I'd been so physically attracted to anyone. Babel's nostrils flared with a slight huff. His brows narrowed. His eyes dark with purpose. I felt like Little Red Riding Hood, and Babel filled the role of the Big Bad Wolf intent on eating my goody basket. Oh, if only.

Pull yourself together, Sunny. But it was really hard, along with his arms, his chest, his abs, his...

Holding me tighter, his arms locked around me. He stroked my back with his firm hands. I trembled, fighting back a deep moan. "Please let me up, Babel," I said again.

He froze for a second then relaxed. He unlocked his arms from around me and smiled. "Call me Babe. Everybody does."

To say I scrambled off his body would be a bit of an overstatement. The trembling had left my arms and knees weak, but I managed, albeit slowly. "I don't know you well enough to call you Babe. Sorry." I couldn't keep my eyes off his semi-erect package.

"Could you put some clothes on? I'm feeling a little..."

He propped up on an elbow like a *Playgirl* centerfold and grinned. "Overdressed?"

What an egomaniac! "No. Sheesh." Okay, so maybe I felt a tad overdressed, even in my pink spaghetti-strap shirt dress with black short-shorts and sandals. It was hot in Missouri. Sticky hot. And besides, I'd put in more hours than I care to count at the gym to counterbalance my donut habit, so I deserved to wear those shorts. My exercise routine wasn't all about the donuts. Over a year of no sex, since the dickhead had cheated, and while I'm no sex maniac, that's a long time for someone who had been getting it on the reg.

The "no sex" could also explain why I had such a visceral reaction to this guy. No doubt the man was a hunka-hunka. "Could you quit posing on the floor?" I wagged my finger toward his poker. "And for the love of daisies, put some clothes on before that thing puts out someone's eye."

He had the courtesy to look the tiniest bit embarrassed. "Nothing personal. It's a purely physical reaction."

"I'm sure you say that to all the girls."

"Sorry, I just meant, well, I'm a guy. You brush against the junk, it goes stiff."

"And here I thought I was special." This line of conversation bordered on hurting my feelings. I know I'm not a beauty queen, but neither am I Medusa. "You can shut up now."

Color rose to his cheeks—those nice fuzzy, chiseled, scruffy, manly cheeks, so perfectly bookending his Roman nose and gorgeous bow lips. And damn it to hell, his teeth were friggin' perfect! He pulled himself up by grabbing the counter, and holy schmoly, the man was tall. If I had to guess, he bordered on 6'5". I'm pretty sure I hated him for being so beautifully handsome.

"I only meant to say..."

I almost offered to buy him a shovel, but he managed to dig his own hole quite deep without any help from me. "I've got it already, jeesh. Not interested, physical reaction, yadda, yadda, yadda. No need to explain yourself further. Besides, I'm not looking for a boyfriend, so doesn't matter. And even if I were, it certainly wouldn't be my best friend's baby brother. We cool?" I didn't wait for him to answer. I waved him off. "Great. Excellent. Awesome even. Now, put on some damn clothes." Why-oh-why was I attracted to crazy?

"Perhaps you could find me a diaper."

Guess he didn't like the "baby" comment. Oh well. Sucks to be him.

He covered himself with his hands. Thank God. However, it didn't stop me from checking out the rest of his body. *Ay Chihuahua!* Damn, it kind of sucked to be me.

I knew from Chav that Babel had moved back to

Kansas City where their parents lived after he'd taken a year off from university to look for their brother Judah. What was he still doing here? A horrible thought entered my head. "If you're here, does that mean..."

His face suddenly sobered. "I don't know. Mom and Dad haven't been able to get ahold of her for the last couple of days, so they sent me down to check in. I got here yesterday."

"She texted me a couple of days ago. I haven't been able to get ahold of her since then." I lifted a hand to comfort him, but his nakedness stopped me from breaching the distance. "Babel, we're going to find her." Even if I had to turn over every stump and stone in this backward-ass town.

"Call me Babe. Everyone does."

That was the second time he'd said that to me, but I couldn't call him Babe. No way, no how. Too intimate. Especially since I'd seen him in his birthday suit. "I don't think so."

He chuckled, low and sexy, and everything went right south of my navel. "Sunny, I'm afraid I've, err...lost my clothes."

"You've got to be kidding me." How did a person go about losing all their damn clothes? "Fine. I'll stay on one side of the counter. You stay on the other. Kapeesh?"

"I understand," he said with a practiced tolerance. It made me wonder who he'd gotten so much practice with.

He hadn't turned around yet, and part of me felt really sad about it. I'm sure he had a killer butt to go with his killer bod. I was all about the teeth and ass. But there were no complaints about the whole frontal part of him either, so...

"Good. Should I call someone for you? Or do you want to call someone? A girlfriend? Anyone who can bring you some clothes?" Subtle. Not.

"The phone's not working here even if I could call someone."

I noticed he'd didn't say "no girlfriend." Much to my annoyance, I cared. And why was the phone turned off? "Don't you have a cell phone that works?"

He moved his hands, indicating his lack of attire. "No pockets."

In the immortal words of Homer Simpson, *Doh*! I snuck another quick glance at his dangly bits, even more annoyed with myself for not having better self-control. "Great. Fantastic." I waved my hand again and purposefully looked away. I had a cell phone out in my truck, and was just about to tell him I'd go get it when he stepped out from behind the counter, still full Monty. "Hey! Keep the mammoth covered."

"Flattering. But there's nothing prehistoric about it." He cocked his eyebrow and smirked.

Bastard.

"Look here, darling." He pointed to his "junk" as he'd called it and said, "This here is what you call a penis. It's connected to the bladder and the bladder is full. Turn your head if you want, sweetheart, but I'm heading to the john."

"Lovely. And I'm not your darling." I made a show of rolling my eyes and turning away. "I'm going to get my cell phone. I expect you to be standing behind the counter by the time I get back." Now, for the sake of posterity—well, at least for the sake of his posterior—I glanced back as he headed left to the bathroom. Of course, it was sort of hard to notice his ass when I saw the— "Blood..." I whispered.

A pain pierced my temple as my knees buckled beneath me. I dropped to the ground. My peripheral vision narrowed to black. The pounding of blood racing through my arteries swelled loudly in my ears. It was out of beat with my heart.

The thumping of blood stopped, my eyesight began to clear, and I was in Babel's arms.

"Sunny? You okay?" I heard his voice as a muffled echo.

No, I wanted to tell him. I wasn't okay. But my mouth didn't work. A vision came over me. I could sense it like death come knocking. Then I was no longer in Babel's arms. I was a ghost. A spectator.

I was...in a shabby apartment with furniture dating back to the seventies? Had I traveled to the past? It wasn't unheard of for me, but it couldn't be relevant for something in my life now since I hadn't been born until 1974. Or could it? Great. The powers that be were giving me a psychic reading on my lost Crissy doll. Useless.

I heard a muffled cry, maybe a scream from beyond the front door. I passed through and down the stairs. The noise grew louder. Animalistic growls and snarls. Fear tightened in my stomach.

It's not real, I reminded myself several times as the feral sounds made me shiver.

I couldn't see any creature, but it certainly sounded like someone was getting voraciously attacked. And the room—it looked familiar. Two windows high up on the far wall spilled moonlight across the floor to...the counter? This was the restaurant. The noise continued, loud, animalistic, with grunting, groaning, and a masculine "ah!" Oh. Oh no.

If I'd really been there, I'd have run, but the vision took me closer to the scene of the crime. On the floor, behind the counter, a gorgeous woman with long dark hair, golden eyes, and even in the bad lighting, a body I'd give my right tit for, straddled the very naked and very sexy Babel Trimmel. I wanted to gouge out my eyes. Where was a hot poker salesman when you needed him?

The woman threw her head back and laughed. "You were fantastic, Babe. As always."

He smiled, his eyes rolling back a little. Coming up on his elbows, he leaned his left shoulder forward and looked behind. "You've got to do something about those fingernails."

"Just marking my territory."

Holy smack, the blood on the floor had happened during sexcapades? Yikes.

"I'm not your territory, Sheila."

The woman, Sheila apparently, picked up a bottle of Canadian Mist from the floor beside them, took a swig, then dumped some of the amber liquid down his large chest. No wonder the place reeked.

Babel shook his head and gave her thigh a light slap. "It's time to go, Sheila. I've got to get the place cleaned up."

"You sure you don't want to move here?" She licked his nipple. "I've sure missed you."

He sighed. The sigh sounded like it'd been one that he'd perfected over and over for this very argument. "It's not this town or you. I've got a real life out there." *He said "there" as though he* was talking about an alien planet. "I'm going to find my sister, then get back to it."

"And what if you don't find her?" Sheila asked. "You never found Judah."

Babel's eyes narrowed. "Not an option," he said. Then added, "I'm finding her, and after, getting the heck out of this town. It's brought nothing but bad luck for my family."

"Sorry," she said, as if she wasn't sorry, an evil smile playing on her lips. Okay, so maybe more mischievous than evil, but it was my vision, I could use whatever adjectives I liked. "But you know that answer pisses me off."

Before he could blink, she whacked him super hard across the temple with the bottle of blended whiskey, and Babel was out like a light.

"Bastard," Sheila muttered. Which I understood, because it had been my sentiment exactly.

She dressed quickly, gathered up Babel's clothes, and walked into the kitchen area. It was small, but nice. I hadn't had a chance to see it yet, so it was like my very own psychic tour. She opened the walk-in freezer and chucked the jeans, boots, socks, and T-shirt inside. No underwear. Huh. I'd file that nugget away for later.

My vision stopped with her slamming the front door, and suddenly I was back, looking up from the floor at the towering and still very naked Babel. "Ow." My head, my back, my butt—everything hurt. "Did you drop me?"

"What the hell just happened?" He looked a little freaked out.

I got up on my elbows and rubbed the back of my skull. "Did you drop me on the ground?"

"You were having a seizure or something. I laid you on

221

the floor." He was definitely freaked. "If I'd had a phone I'd have called for the doc, but..."

"I'm fine now. You can stop worrying." I moved my feet off the chair Babel had propped them up on.

"I'm sorry. I'm squeamish about blood."

Which wasn't a complete lie. Blood tended to bring on funky psychic mojo that left me drained and pained. Although, I'll admit, these visions had been much stronger than normal. Apparently, Chavvah wasn't the only Trimmel who put my psychic stuff on speed dial.

"I'm getting that about you." At least he sounded less upset.

I closed my eyes. "Why would you let someone do that to your back?"

"That's a story for another day, darlin'."

Yeah, I knew the story. Not so sure I wanted the blow-by-blow again. I felt his arms go under me, and I opened my eyes, staring into the deep abyss of his gorgeous, Midwest baby blues.

I let him carry me upstairs to the apartment. I'm not a small woman, but he held me like I weighed next to nothing, which made me think kindlier of him. With my arms around his shoulders, I could smell an unidentifiable musk and spice to his skin. He sat me down on a couch—the scent went from musky to musty—then he went into another room. I heard water running in the sink. More than a whisper of regret passed through me. I barely knew the man and I missed being in his arms. I looked around the living room.

This was the seventies place where my vision had started. The retro decor lacked any sophistication that could've made the space sensational. I knew this had been where Judah lived when he'd been in town. He'd rented this building before his disappearance, and Chav had used our stake to purchase it during her search for him. His vanishing had hit her hard.

Chav told me once that she hadn't agreed with her oldest brother's "lifestyle choice," but she respected him. I'd asked her what she meant, but she had shaken her head, unwilling to elaborate. I knew it wasn't as simple as him being gay or anything like that, because Chav, like myself, was socially liberal. Hell, she'd have started her own PFLAG (Parents, Families, and Friends of Lesbians and Gays) in Peculiar if that had been the case. No. There was something else she hadn't approved of.

I heard the water turn off in the kitchen. Babel returned and proceeded to wipe my face and neck with a cool cloth.

"There now, all better." For a second, he sounded like my father. Which totally squicked me, considering the hard-core fantasies I had about him. He put the wash-cloth in my hand and patted my shoulder. "I'm going to jump in the shower real quick. I'll be back in a few."

Part of me wanted to watch him walk away strictly for the view, but since that part seemed to have done gone and lost its damn mind, I waited until I heard water running before looking in his direction.

He'd left the bathroom door open. Perv.

I couldn't believe it, less than an hour in a new town and I'd witnessed a *Red Shoe Diary* moment, and the star was lathering up less than ten feet away. I would've been downright disgusted by the whole morning if I hadn't been so preoccupied with thoughts of slippery suds sliding along his perfectly formed pecs. (Now I understand how bad porn gets started. Bow chick-a bow-wow.)

I will not go stare at the naked man. I repeated this mantra in my head over and over as I ran down the stairs to the kitchen.

Grabbing his clothes from the freezer, I contemplated where they'd been and how they got there as I carried them back upstairs. They were cold and held the scent of sweat, but at least he'd have something to put on so he could go away. I placed them on the couch, and dear Lord, it was a really ugly couch. It would be the first piece of furniture to go when Chav and I started fixing the place up. And with that thought, I went downstairs to wait for him.

Fifteen minutes later, the light flickered on in the stairwell. Babel's arms and face glistened with dewy goodness as he walked down the steps. He rubbed a tea towel, barely big enough to dry a fish's butt, against his loose mane of wet hair. His blue T-shirt clung to his chest. Water soaking through the fabric made spots the color of midnight.

He must have felt me staring, because he dropped his arm to his side and looked at me. "Where'd you find my clothes?"

"The freezer." I wrapped my knuckle on the counter. "Guess you can go home now."

"Guess so." He shrugged as he stretched his body to tuck in his shirt. "But we should probably talk."

"I'm in no mood." *For talk.* Damn, he was super-fine.

"Well, you kind of need to get in the mood." He shook

his hair out, droplets spraying out around him. It began to feel like a bad (or really good, depending on who you asked) shampoo commercial. "There's been a mistake. My sister should've never invited you out here, Sunny."

"You've said that already, but unfortunately for you, my name's on the property, same as hers, all legal and binding. I'm staying. Period. End of discussion. Besides, I'm not going anywhere until I find Chav."

Babel chewed his lower lip and narrowed his eyes at me. "I don't think you understand the situation."

"Oh, I think I do. You don't like me. Fine. I get that."

"It's a might more complicated than that." He scratched at his five o'clock shadow.

I resisted the temptation to offer him a hand. "Why do you care, anyway? Don't you have a *real* life you want to get back to? You seem awfully concerned for a guy who isn't even sticking around."

"And what makes you think that?" Babel asked.

"Uh..." Fair question. I couldn't exactly tell him that I'd heard him tell his cuh-razy lover in a vision. "Well, you didn't exactly stick around after the search was called off for Judah."

A pained expression crossed his face. I instantly regretted being such an ass. It was a low blow, and petty even.

"I stayed for as long as I could stand it." He shook his head. "I'm not meant for this place, Sunny. And neither are you."

Another twinge. "It doesn't matter." We would find Chavvah, then he would be gone. "Have you heard anything? Are the police searching for her?"

"No and yes. I haven't heard from Chavvie, but Sheriff Taylor isn't giving up." He flicked his thumbnail against his ring fingernail. "Not yet, anyways."

"She'll show up, Babel. I just know it." But I didn't know it. In my heart, I believed she was alive, and not because of any vision. "She's my best friend. I'd feel it if she was gone. Now, go on back to wherever you're staying..." Oh, crap. Maybe he'd been staying here. "You do have another place to stay don't you?"

Babel nodded once. "I've been staying at Chavvie's cabin down by the lake."

"Good," I whispered. I'd want to check out her place later for clues to what happened. "It's been a long drive for me, and I need a nap so I can figure out what I have to do next to find her."

He shook his head as if he was having an argument with himself. "I'll be back in a couple of hours with some cleaning supplies and get the floor behind the counter scrubbed."

I didn't want to talk anymore. I wanted to get my bags out of the truck. I'd hassle with unpacking the U-Haul later, but the bags were a must. I needed something personal, something of mine in this place. I held out my hand. "That's a nice offer. I can manage. Thanks."

Babel took my hand, and gave me a tight-lipped smile. "You don't handle blood very well. After I clean it up, maybe we can compare notes about Chavvie."

I nodded, afraid that if I spoke the dams would open and I wouldn't be able to stop the tears. Then I heard a voice like a whisper in my ear.

Save her.

Babel let go of my hand. "I'll be back." The way he said it sounded more like a threat than a promise. As he walked out the front door, he added, "You've got an audience."

Get this book from your favorite eTailer!

PRAISE FOR RENEE GEORGE

"Grimoires of a Middle Aged Witch is my new favorite series! I want a gnome named Linda of my own. Trust me. Read the series. You will not regret a single delightfully hilarious and heartwarming moment.

- Robyn Peterman, NYT and USA Today Bestselling Author of Good to the Last Death series.

"I love Renee's books, and recommend any of her series! They catch me right up and keep me turning those pages."

~Yasmine Galenorn, New York Times Bestselling Author

"Renee George has crafted a fantastic start to this magical midlife adventure. Pick up Earth Spells Are Easy today! You won't be disappointed."

~Dakota Cassidy, USA Today Bestselling Author

"I'm loving the Paranormal Women's Fiction genre! Renee George's humor shines when a woman of a certain age sniffs out the bad guy and saves her bestie. Funny, strong female friendships rule!"

-- Michelle M. Pillow, NYT & USAT Bestselling Author

ABOUT THE AUTHOR

I am a USA Today Bestselling author who writes paranormal mysteries and romances because I love all things whodunit, Otherworldly, and weird. Also, I wish my pittie, the adorable Kona Princess Warrior and my two cats Ash and Simon could talk. Or at least be more like Scooby-Doo and help me unmask villains at the haunted house up the street.

When I'm not writing about mystery-solving were-cougars or the adventures of a hapless psychic living among shapeshifters, I am preyed upon by stray kittens who end up living in my house because I can't say no to those sweet, furry faces. (Someone stop telling them where I live!)

I live in Mid-Missouri with my family and I spend my non-writing time doing really cool stuff...like watching TV and cleaning up dog poop

Follow Renee!
Bookbub
Renee's Rebel Readers FB Group
Newsletter